THE COWBOY CHRONICLES

The adventures of JR and Lefty

R. Dalton Seawolf

Amazon

To all those who have gone before. To all those who are still here. Long live Cowboys

CONTENTS

PREFACE

Most folks believe cowboys are a thing of the past. I'm not talking about "truckers" calling themselves cowboys, or "country singer" type cowboys, (apparently nowadays, anybody who believes themselves to be an outlaw, or somethin' special are also called "cowboy", for some idiotic reason that escapes me at the moment.) No, I'm talkin' about sure enuff, 100%, true blue, no foolin', bronc stompin', steer ropin', heck raisin,' dyed in the wool cowboys.

Well, I am here to tell you a story of two of the most "cowboy" cowboys who ever shook a loop or set a saddle, and I swear that everything I tell you is true, except for the parts that aren't.

JR and Lefty were pals from the time they could walk. Both grew up in southern New Mexico, (for the uninformed, only real cowboys come from New Mexico, no matter what the people that hail from the state east of us may say,) and both were riding by the age of three, and raisin' heck from there on after. It's not that they were lookin' for trouble; It's just that trouble seemed to always find them.

They lived in a quiet southern New Mexico Village where the culture was Hispanic in every sense of the word. They both learned to speak Spanish and English because most everyone in town did as well. Lefty's father was Tomas Ortiz. He had been the City Marshall as long as anyone could remember. JR's Father Cillian was a rancher who ran cattle on a 60-section ranch that had been in the Reilly family for generations. Lefty and JR's fathers were also childhood friends, which was a bit of a Catch 22, in that they were fully aware of the havoc the younger duo could wreak.

Rather than give you a detailed (and boring) description of the two youngsters, I thought it better to simply let the stories speak for themselves. Trust me, by the time I'm through, you will know them well.

Take, for instance, the day that JR and Lefty rode old Blue jay, the neighbor's mule, into town. Now, both boys were raised in Christian households, with typical Christian values of "do unto others", "honesty in all things" etc. You get the drift. However, to JR and Lefty's way of thinkin', they weren't stealing a mule. They just figured it was easier to ask forgiveness rather than get permission.

To the farmer who owned the mule, however, it was another story. Now old Blue Jay (the mule) was as cantankerous an animal that ever lived. The fact was he liked to stay in the shade at one end of the pasture and hated to move even a few feet away from feed, water, or shade. Given the old mules' predilections, it made it especially hard to get him motivated to walk the two miles required to accomplish their goal, i.e., get to town. The first two attempts at leading the old cuss to the other end of the pasture resulted in the mule making a mad dash back to where he started, both boys clinging for dear life, then being ejected from the "hurricane deck" when he made a sudden stop in front of the water trough.

Now, these two boys weren't much for giving up on an idea once it took hold, and so on the 3rd attempt at their mission they came up with a foolproof plan. The farmer (who will remain anonymous to protect the ignorant), had cut down some mesquite bushes he had then piled next to the fence at the shady end of the pasture to dry.

The idea was that JR would tie a rope around a big mesquite bush, douse it with gasoline and tie the other end to ole' blue jays' tail. Running down to the other end of the pasture, Lefty would open the gate. After the tasks were accomplished and both were securely mounted, JR struck a match and lit the mesquite afire, and waited for Blue jay to run out the gate and on into town.

While the grand scheme worked out well on paper, the outcome was completely different. Instead of running out the gate, Blue jay started bucking and braying, jumped the fence and, with the mesquite full ablaze, ran towards the barn that was filled with well cured (meaning really, really, dry) hay that was promptly ignited and the conflagration (so rare is the opportunity to use conflagration in a sentence) that it lit the henhouse, well house, and assorted other lesser structures on fire. The last the boys saw of Blue Jay, he was headed south to Mexico, where I trust he still lives to this day.

Now, the proper thing to do for these pair of six-year-old's was confess their sins to the farmer, and they would have done just that, if not because everyone was completely convinced that the hay barn had spontaneously combusted (as everyone warned might happen...after the fact) thus, creating the ensuing calamity, as well as redirecting causation away from the true culprits.

Now that farmer had need from time to time of hired hands to help pick cotton, Chile or whatever crop was in season at the moment. JR and Lefty hired on with the farmer to pick cotton, dump it in a cotton trailer, pack it by stomping on it and then, when the cotton trailer was full, the farmer would haul it to the cotton gin.

JR and Lefty worked one day until they had a fully packed trailer and, never ones to remain idle, decided that they would hook up the trailer to the farmer's truck and take it to the gin themselves.

Now, in the country, youngsters learn to drive as soon as they can reach the pedals. The problem was that a couple of eight-year-old's weren't of sufficient height to work the pedals and drive at the same time.

The plan was for JR to drive and shift gears, and Lefty would work the clutch and the brakes and gas.

Now, the particular field where they had picked the cotton was only accessible one way, and that way was down an irrigation ditch that was running full of water. As anyone who has seen an irrigation canal will know, driving on top of the levee is sketchy and downright suicidal at worst, for even an experienced driver. Of course, these inconvenient facts never crossed either of the boy's minds.

As JR and Lefty put their plan into action, they were grinning ear to ear at the thought of how happy the farmer would be because of their ingenuity. Slowly at first, the truck pulled onto the canal levee, and everything was going pretty well.

While the reader may have assumed at the outset that

Lefty was called Lefty because he was lefthanded; such was not the case. Lefty was called Lefty because he had a hard time remembering which was left and which was right. (It occurs to me he could have been nicknamed Righty, but that is just plain silly.)

As the truck motor RPM's wound up to the speed to shift into second gear, JR hollered, "Ok Lefty, put in the clutch, it's the one on the left". Lefty thought carefully and for once got it …right, but too far right. Punching the gas pedal, the truck lurched forward, which caused it to veer to the right. JR over corrected to the left, which caused the trailer to jackknife and roll into the brim-full canal. The cotton quickly absorbed water, swelled, and dammed up the canal, which then began overflowing into neighboring fields.

For many years after, the townsfolk were heard to say that instead of being known as the "Chile Capital of the World", the town slogan should have been "Home of the World's Biggest Tampon."

As is certainly appropriate, JR and Lefty did not get away with this fiasco Scot free, and it was decided that they both would work to reimburse the farmer, until the full value of the cotton was paid for; it took them quite a few cotton seasons to accomplish.

Time went on with only minor infractions and before anyone knew it, JR and Lefty had graduated from High School and on to university, where they tried out for the rodeo team. By this time, Lefty and JR had done all the growing they were going to' do, and both boys turned into right handsome and physically stout specimens of western men.

JR was tall at 6'3", Lefty fell in at about 5'10", but was

broad shouldered and stout as a bull. Because riding "wooly" broncs was second nature to them, JR and Lefty were soon traveling around to various University rodeos ridin' the hair off every saddle bronc they came across, and this is where the proper story begins.

CHAPTER 1:
RODEO HANDS

Because the college rodeo circuit was not a "paid gig", JR and Lefty got permitted by the Professional Rodeo Cowboys Association (PRCA.) Now, to enter rodeos that paid real money, the pair had to win a certain dollar amount, which is called "filling your card", before you can compete professionally. But there are a few rodeos, like the Calgary Stampede, where a couple of enterprising young fellers could enter a specialty event, … such as wild cow milking (not a joke), that did not require a PRCA card.

Now this event required three individuals; one to mug the cow, one to tail the cow, and one to milk the cow. What the reader needs to understand is that when something is called "wild cow milking", we aren't talking about a Holstein cow from a diary that looks forward to being relieved of a full udder. We are talking about a cow off the range who probably has only seen a human twice in its entire life. Another thing, we aren't talking about an 800-pound heifer, we are talking about a 1,800 pound full grown horned cow who is in a foul mood on her best day, and would be profoundly offended at anyone fooling with her milking parts on any day.

The problem was; where were they going to find someone who will take the "cow by the horns," literally? You see, JR and Lefty had already decided who was gonna tail and who was gonna milk. They just needed someone of below average intellect to do the mugging.

"Lefty, I just had a brainstorm."

"Did you mean brain fart JR? because I have never known you to be a brainstorm kinda guy."

"Everyone knows I'm the brains and you're the brawn of this outfit, so shut up and let me tell you my plan."

"Ok, I'm listening."

"You remember that kid who tried out for the rodeo team and hung up in the stirrup and nearly got stomped to death?"

"I remember he had a tough time forming useful words after the incident. What about him?"

"Let me tell you, that kid is tougher than the back wall of a shooting gallery. He was back at it the next day after his unfortunate debacle" (picture in your mind JR with a Cheshire cat grin because of his use of a twenty-dollar word.)

"I bet he will do it for sure."

"Well, you can ask him, but I won't hold my breath."

Wonder of wonders, Joe Langford was all in. According to Lefty, Joe's inability to speak must have been temporary because the boy just would not shut up the entire trip to Calgary, Alberta, Canada.

"Joe?" Lefty queried, "when you were a kid, did they ever make you ride in the back of the pickup truck on long trips?"

"Gosh yeah!" Joe laughed.

"If you don't quit talking, I'm gonna throw you in the back of the truck and see how long it takes for you to become a human popsicle."

Joe quit talking, leaned back in the seat, and sulked.

"Now Lefty, you shouldn't be so hard on the kid. After all, he is one third of the reason that we are gonna make some money this weekend."

"If you don't shut up, JR, I'll put you back there with him."

"Forgive Lefty Joe, he suffers from an inability to connect with his feminine side, and it causes him to lash out. I have been trying to get him to come out of the closet, but he refuses to acknowledge it."

"Did you just call me gay?"

Joe and JR laughed until their sides ached. Of all the things Lefty was, he was certainly not gay. This time it was Lefty's turn to sulk.

JR and Lefty had almost come to blows a few times in their life, but the only reason they hadn't was because neither one of them knew who would win. One of their past times was "hacking" on each other. Someone who didn't know them would swear they hated each other, but the fact of the matter was, they would take a bullet for each other.

Take the time when a couple of Chollos cornered JR in a bar and tried to rearrange his face. Lefty turned into the Hulk and pounded both of them until JR had to pull him off for fear he would kill them. JR never even got a punch in. Lefty told the two Chollos lying bleeding on the floor, "You touch my brother again, and you are dead." He wasn't kidding.

Driving straight through to Calgary from New Mexico took almost two days. By the time they got to the arena, they were all three played out, but they had no time to rest before the big event. Now, the Calgary arena is huge. We're talking football field hugely. And what made it even worse, for the wild cow milking contest, all the cowboys, and all the cows, were all in the same place at the same time. The only thing keeping the cows from running off to the opposite end of the arena one hundred yards away were a couple of mounted cowboys that kept them pushed in a corner until the announcer said, "get your cow!"

All at once, ten cowboys run out to grab any of 20 head of cows and milk them. Now, it wasn't required that you milk a bucket full. All you had to do was get a couple of squirts of milk into a coke bottle. To the uninformed, a couple of squirts of milk seem simple enough. However, if you permit me, I will attempt to form an analogy to create an accurate image in your mind of what it is like to milk a wild cow. Imagine, if you will, that you are asked to fill a teacup. Simple right? Now imagine that you see yourself with a teacup in one hand, and a teapot in the other, filling the teacup, while you are in the middle of a category five hurricane! That just about covers it.

"Ok Joe, here is the plan. You need to grab the cow you think would be the easiest to milk. Lefty will grab her by the tail, and I'll milk her, and run like a house afire to the finish line; got it?" Joe grinned and nodded his head, but to Lefty, it looked like Joe was a bit confused. Just then the announcer yelled, "get your cow!" Joe ran to the herd and stood there for a second, then ran right over to the biggest cow, with the biggest set of horns there ever was.

Now, these horns turned straight up like a buffalo's do; not a good thing.

JR hollered for Joe to pick another, but it was too late. All Lefty and JR could do was follow Joe's lead. Joe wrapped his arms around the cows horns, Lefty grabbed the tail and, as if the cow never even knew there was a couple cowboys hanging on her, sucked back behind Joe, rammed a horn right up poor old joes tail pipe a good 6 inches, then made a run for it to the other end of the arena, with Joe impaled on her horn howling like a banshee, Lefty holding her tail, and JR running alongside with the coke bottle at the ready.

Before anyone gets the idea that this was a total disaster, keep in mind that after a contestant got a couple of squirts of milk in the bottle, he had to be the first to run to the other end of the arena and across the finish line. Fortunately for Joe, Lefty, and JR, the cow did the running for all three of them, and by a stroke of luck, JR could get a couple of squirts of milk in the bottle, because the cow was preoccupied with the cowboy stuck on her horn, and forgot about what was happening behind her, just as they crossed the finish line... first.

There were a few disgruntled cowboys on the opposing teams that viewed Lefty and JR's method of a winning scornfully, but the judges concluded that because of the unfortunate de-flowering of Joe by the cow, that they would let it slide. After the cow and Joe were successfully separated, Joe spent the night in the hospital, where they discovered that except for some bruising, there was no major damage done, and he was released the next day. Joe flew home, and Lefty and JR never saw him again. The boys just figured he wised up about rodeo... it ain't for everyone.

On the way back to New Mexico, the boys passed through Murray, Utah, and as luck would have it, the Saddle Bronc event at the Murray Rodeo had a high number of entrants, meaning more money in the jackpot, so Lefty entered the contest.

The horse Lefty drew was an exceptionally rough bronc, and as was JR's custom, he coached Lefty on how to ride, which always ended with Lefty either kicking him, or throwing something at him, to get him to shut up.

"Let me have him boys," Lefty called out when the worst thing that could happen ...happened. The horse reared straight up in the air and came down on top of Lefty while still in the chute. After what seemed like a lifetime, the gate attendants opened the gate, and the horse rolled off Lefty, who was honking like a goose because the breath was knocked out of him. What is more, lefty was paralyzed from the waist down ... or so he thought. As the medics loaded Lefty on the gurney to take him to the hospital, he reached up and grabbed JR by the arms and said, "I can't live paralyzed JR. you are gonna have to shoot me, I mean it, I can't live like this."

"Don't worry Lefty, I'll do it." He pronounced resolutely.

A few hours later, Lefty had the feeling back in his legs, and was sleeping soundly. He heard a noise and opened one eye to see JR standing over him with a 38 revolver, sniffling and trying to hold back the tears, drunker than Cooter Brown.

"JR don't shoot, I'm ok." Lefty yelled.

"No, you're not Lefty. You're just saying that to spare my feelings."

"No JR, seriously! I'm ok now see?"

Lefty got up from the bed and, with his hospital gown gaping open, then danced the jig to prove he could walk.

"Well ... if you're sure. I couldn't find any bullets, anyway. I was thinkin' about just beatin' you to death with the pistol"

JR was so drunk that he collapsed onto a chair and was fast asleep snoring like a freight train in less than a minute. Lefty pried the pistol out of his hand and went back to bed.

CHAPTER 2: WORKING COWBOYS

Having all the fun they could stand for now; JR and Lefty headed back home and get work on the Benton ranch in the Boot Heel of New Mexico.

He and Lefty would have rather worked on JR's own spread, but the boys needed cash, and JR's dad Cillian Reilly figured that a place to sleep, and three meals was adequate payment, or in his own words "owners' equity" in that it would be JR and Lefty's someday.

The winter in southern New Mexico was closing in fast, making rolling out of bed even harder than normal. JR and Lefty had worked cattle all their lives, and it was a source of humor for them to read reports in the news that "cowboyin'" was a thing of the past, and real cowboys didn't exist anymore. Tell that to the hundreds of New Mexico ranchers and ranch hands, who worked their entire life pushing cattle around pastures, risking life and limb every day. Sure, the ranching in New Mexico wasn't as big as it once was, but there still were plenty of opportunities to "cowboy" if you really wanted to.

"You up yet JR?"

"What the heck do you think? I woke up hours ago thinking there was a bear in the camp. Dang son! How in the heck do you sleep through that dangdable snoring?"

"I wasn't snoring, you ignorant fool. I was dreaming I was a motorcycle," JR laughed aloud.

JR and Lefty had been friends since they were toddlers. JR grew up tall and good looking, but Lefty, well, let's just say that what Lefty lacked in stature and looks, he made up in strength and hard-headedness. Whatever trouble JR got into, Lefty could usually pull him out. He was quick with his fists and not afraid to swing 'em. JR was more of a lover than a fighter; the reason that he got into trouble most everywhere he went.

Cowboy bars were a hunting ground for JR. He didn't much care if a girl had a boyfriend or not, that just made the chase more exciting. The one thing that both had in common was a love of the cowboy life ... and roping. JR was a champion header, and Lefty was one of the best heelers in the country. Whenever they ran short of cash, it was a sure-fire way to get healed up ... financially speaking, that is. Problem was that most ranchers frowned on anyone roping their cattle. They wanted them moved around gently so they wouldn't run off any weight. The only way a cowboy could use his rope these days was on sick cattle or a wayward steer that needed a tune up. JR and Lefty seemed to find plenty that needed treatment.

"I'm gonna ride that grullo colt today", JR said.

"Leave it to you to ride the worst bronc we have on a wintry morning like today", Lefty replied.

"What don't kill you will strengthen you? What you have failed to grasp is that you must test yourself every day, otherwise you'll get soft."

"Well, I think you're soft in the head, and that's why you're always lookin' for trouble.

The fact of the matter was, both Lefty and JR had ridden broncs all their life, and both went to the University on rodeo scholarships, making it to the College National Finals riding saddle bronc all four years, and then professionally with the PRCA after that. But the money just wasn't there in saddle bronc … roping was the moneymaker.

Roger Denton walked out of his ranch house and headed down to the barn to check on his hired hands. He considered himself fortunate having JR Reilly and Lefty Ortiz working for him. The pay was not great, and the workday was from "can to can't," seven days a week, but Lefty and JR were motivated by tradition and love of the lifestyle, more than just dollars and cents. It was hard enough making a living ranching these days even with their help; without them helping, he couldn't make it at all … leads a man to do things he never thought he would just to survive.

Benton never had to worry about getting the job done right. His only worry was keeping JR away from his 23-year-old daughter Elise … a full-time job.

"You boys ready to head out?"

"Yes sir, me and Lefty are gonna head out to the picacho pasture and gather those brimmer steers … if I can get Lefty off his butt."

"If you're waiting on me, son, you're backing up. I've been ready for the last hour while you take the kinks out of that bronc you're riding."

"Why in the heck are you riding that colt JR? Feeling a little froggy this morning?"

"Yes sir, I was just explaining to Lefty here that if you don't test yourself, every day, you'll get soft and wimpy. You might have observed the beginning symptoms in Lefty there."

"Once again, my friend JR's mouth is writing checks his butt can't cash … the day that this white boy out works, out rides, or outperforms me, will be the day that pigs fly. I taught him everything he knows, but I don't like to make a big deal out of my abilities for fear of discouraging the poor boy."

"You boys better ride out before the BS gets too deep."

"Yes sir, Mr. Benton," they replied in unison as they kicked their horses into a lope, heading north to the pasture.

Benton chuckled to himself, thinking about his hired hands. He had known them since they were boys and they had always needled each other relentlessly. They were closer than brothers, and he pitied anyone who got in between them. There is nothing they wouldn't do for each other … despite the constant trash talking they heaped on one another.

JR was tall and handsome. Lefty was a few inches shorter, with a bodybuilder's physique. While Lefty was a good-looking kid in his own right, JR usually got most of the attention.

Benton walked towards his pickup to head for town to talk to the banker when his daughter, Elise, came walking from the house.

"Hi dad, has JR left yet?" she asked coyly.

"You don't be worrying about that Reilly kid. He is too worldly for you."

"Mom said that you were just like him when you were young … you turned out alright didn't you?"

"That is beside the point… I'm headed to town. Care to ride along?"

"No thanks. I'm gonna saddle up that buckskin mare and go help with the roundup."

"That's fine, but you stay out of JR and Lefty's way … I don't want you distracting them."

Elise Benton was indeed a distraction. She was tall with dark hair and green eyes, the spitting image of her mother, who was Hispanic. In cowboy parlance, Benton and his wife made a "good cross," as displayed by Elise, who was a true beauty. Benton was a little overly protective, probably because he was a cowboy, and familiar with a cowboys' intentions. The thing was, Elise could take care of herself, and she was definitely picky about her suitors. The problem was that she never gave a city boy a second look. She was attracted to cowboys, and the more cowboy, the better ... not always a good thing.

A few hours later, JR and Lefty had the pasture gathered and were trailing over two hundred head of yearling Brahma cross steers, south towards the corrals at the ranch headquarters. JR's bronc colt broke in half five times, bucking and twisting to dislodge its rider. JR rode out the storm every time but couldn't understand why that danged horse wouldn't warm up and go to work.

"What the heck, JR? that horse acts like it has a burr under its blanket."

"I checked twice and adjusted the cinch. We ought a think about selling the rascal to a rodeo contractor."

JR didn't know it, but Lefty had a slingshot in his vest pocket, and whenever JR wasn't looking, he would shoot a rock and hit the horse in the rear end that sent him off on another tangent.

"Nah ... I think he will come out of it ... just give it time", Lefty chuckled.

As in every herd of young steers, there was always a rebel

in the crowd. Every so often, a determined steer would make a break for it and try to get back to where it came from. Rather than irritate JR and Lefty, it gave them an opportunity to give chase and rope the rascal and encourage him to comply.

An ornery steer decided it would not be persuaded and took off with Lefty in hot pursuit. The steer ran over a hill and along an arroyo that kept him running along the rim. As Lefty shook out a loop and began his throw, the entire world seemed to explode as his horse went down the steep side of the ravine and ended up falling on top of him. Lefty had been in dozens of horse wrecks before, but there was no reason that he could see for the horse collapsing like it did.

JR came riding hard, and fast to check on Lefty who seemed to vanish from view. What he found made his heart skip a beat.

"Dang Lefty, if you needed a nap, you could have said something."

"Thought I could catch a few winks at the bottom of this arroyo and catch up to you later."

"What in heck happened?"

"An old woman taught me how to fly on a horse … I should have paid more attention."

The horse Lefty was riding was absolutely dead. The fall wasn't high enough to cause its death, and as JR helped get his leg out from under it, he soon discovered what happened.

"Lefty, that horse was shot out from under you. "

"What the heck? … You're right, that is a bullet wound. Hit him right at the base of his neck and killed him."

"Are you hurt Lefty?"

"Normally I would never admit it to you, because I would never hear the end of it, but I think my ankle is broken."

Lefty pulled his right boot off and discovered it was a lot worse than he thought. The ankle bone had perforated the skin and, without the pressure of his boot on the foot, it bled profusely.

"I better just put this boot back on to stanch the blood. You might have to leave me here and get the four-wheeler. Walking might be out of the question, and I'll be danged if I ride double."

Without another word, JR kicked the colt into high gear and headed to the ranch headquarters as fast as he could. Before long, he came upon Elise, who was headed out to help JR and Lefty.

"What's wrong? Elise asked with alarm.

Someone shot the horse out from under Lefty, and compound fractured his ankle his ankle when it fell on top of him. He is bleeding badly, and I have to go get the four-wheeler before he bleeds out."

"Where is he?"

"Up along that hill yonder, down in the arroyo."

"I'll help him until you get back." Elise said firmly.

JR was back to help Lefty in little over an hour. He didn't bother to unsaddle or cool his horse out and went right to the four-wheeler and drove as fast as he could. When he arrived at the site of the accident, he noticed the dead horse was unsaddled. Lefty and Elise were laughing as he came up.

"A good cowboy knows never to show weakness in front of a woman … it makes them feel unsafe and insecure", JR thought to himself.

"If you feel well enough to be making jokes, you could have walked out and met me halfway."

"JR, don't you dare needle him right now? His ankle is in

awful shape, and he needs a doctor immediately."

"Yes ma'am", JR mumbled.

After Lefty was admitted to the emergency room, JR made a phone call to Mr.

Benton. He needed to tell him about the shooting incident.

"Mr. Benton, it's JR, I have a spot of trouble I need to tell you about. Lefty went after an ignorant steer to push him back in the herd and his horse fell into an arroyo and broke his ankle."

"The horse broke its ankle?"

"No sir, sorry, Lefty broke his ankle. The horse is dead. When I rolled the horse off of Lefty's leg, we saw a bullet hole from what looked like a high-powered rifle at the base of its neck ... killed him instantly. I reckon it was a hunter who made a stray shot. Can't think that anyone meant to shoot him intentionally."

There was silence on the other end of the line. "Mr. Benton? Are you there?"

Benton's mind was whirling. He could not believe that the threats that the threats made against him would cause this. He couldn't tell JR the truth, so after he composed himself, he continued the conversation.

"I'm here, I'm here ... my phone signal must have dropped for a second. Send any bills from the hospital to me. Tell Lefty that I'll keep him on the payroll no matter what. Just tell him to take it easy ... I'll talk to him later."

"Yes, sir."

"That was curious," JR said aloud.

After the doctor set his ankle, Lefty was ready to leave. Seeing JR in the hallway, he motioned him over with one crutch.

"We need to get the heck out of here, pard."

"You sure you're ready?"

"I'm ready ... we need to get someplace where I can cut this cast off."

"That is by far the most ignorant thing you have ever said! ... Your frickin' bone was hanging out two hours ago. Now you want to undo everything that was done did?"

"Yep ... that about sums it up."

"Alright, but I don't want you pissin' and moanin' about what you should a done.

You remember old Chalk Chapman?"

"Oh, for heck's sake, you aren't gonna 'Chalk Chapman' me, are you?"

"Since it bears on this conversation; I will. Chalk always said that he regretted not taking care of old injuries because by the time he was fifty he could barely walk, use his hands, or salute in the morning."

"Leave it to you to worry about your giggle stick not working. Besides, Chalk got kicked in the cajones by a bull as a kid, that's why his pito didn't work" Lefty almost fell off his crutches laughing.

"You may think it's a small matter", JR said in his best southern drawl, "but it's a serious topic."

"Oh, my heck!" Lefty hooted, "yours IS a small matter!! ...I've seen it."

"Alright idiot, forget I said anything. I hope you die."

Roger Benton lied to his wife. He didn't want to, but he couldn't let her know he was going across the border to Janos, Mexico.

"How long will you be in Roswell, mi amor?" Celina Benton asked. "Just long enough to pick up a check from the auction and make a deal for that Angus bull darlin' ... I'll be back tomorrow evening."

But Benton was not going to Roswell. He was headed south of the border to deal with a much bigger problem that he had gotten himself into. With cattle prices down, the drought, and troubles with the Bureau of Land Management reducing the number of cattle he could graze, Benton was desperate.

Ranching on the border meant dealing with smugglers who used the Little Hatchet mountains as a trade route.

The terrain was so rough it was nigh unto impossible to monitor the area, so the Border Patrol mostly didn't. The problem the smugglers had was moving the drugs from the base of the Little Hatchet mountains to Deming, New Mexico, where they could be divided and redistributed all over the country.

Benton was approached by a drug dealer that needed product moved north on state road 146 and then east on I-10 to Deming. Benton was known in Hidalgo and Luna Counties, so his truck and trailer making frequent trips hauling cattle or horses was not unusual. There were no Border Patrol stops going east, so that wasn't a problem either. Benton was paid $25,000 for each trip... it had kept him in the ranching business for the past three years. He could make the trip in a little over three hours and not be out of communication for any length of time ... it seemed perfect. But things had changed. There were more and more federal law enforcement agents in southern New Mexico, and Benton's conscience was killing him. If he were caught, his wife and daughter would be devastated. He would lose everything, and he just could not do it anymore. Two months ago, he turned down a shipment ... threats were made, and apparently followed through with.

One thing about cowboys and broken bones, they always had a bagful of tricks to defeat cumbersome casts and other medical appliances that impeded "ambulating." Lefty figured he could take his leg cast off, put a high-topped boot on, wrap it with duct tape; tighter around the ankle, of course, and wear it until it healed up. He had done it a few times in the past for broken arms, wrist, ribs, and other bones. It seemed perfectly logical that duct tape would work on an ankle. The only thing he really needed was to get his foot in a stirrup. That meant that the leg cast had to go.

"Alright JR, here is the deal. I need you to get that power saw and adjust it down to where it won't cut any deeper than a half of an inch. I'm gonna prop my leg up on the table, and you're gonna have the honors."

"I don't know, lefty; you remember when you cut the arm cast off me with the hack saw? Didn't work out so well."

"Which is the very reason I want you to use a power saw. Am I the only one who can see the genius in this?"

"I would say that any genius brain cells that you ever had were killed in Cheyenne last year ... Pendleton whiskey is enjoyed, not guzzled like a "Big Gulp.""

"You don't worry about my brain cells; besides, everyone knows that the weakest brain cells are the ones that are killed off first, so for all you know, my head is full of the smartest and best cells there ever was."

JR got the Black and Decker power saw from the tool house and adjusted it down to where just a little blade protruded from the guard.

"Lefty, this is a blade for ripping lumber, don't you think we ought to get something less toothy?"

"You might have a point JR, go see if you can find something with smaller teeth."

After a while, JR returned to the scene of the future surgical procedure with a different tool.

"I found just the thing", Jr said proudly, "A hand grinder with a masonry cutting wheel on it. "

"Now you're thinking, JR, let's get to work."

Meanwhile, back at the ranch house...

"Mom! I'm going to go to the bunkhouse and check on Lefty," Elise called out.

"Don't be long Mija, he needs to get his rest", her mother cautioned.

As Elise arrived at the door of the bunkhouse, she heard loud mechanical noise that made her suspicious.

"JR! what on earth are you doing?" Elise screamed.

"It wasn't my idea Elise; it was the 'brain trust' Lefty who came up with it."

"Don't you realize he has a broken bone and sutures from the compound

Fracture? You could give him blood poisoning, not to mention another deep wound."

"It's ok Elise, I've done it a bunch of times, except this is the first time that we have used power tools," Lefty explained.

"I swear, you two are dumber than a bag of hammers ... you will stop this immediately or I swear I will murder both of you!"

"How do you expect me to work with this thing on?"

"You aren't gonna work ... that's the point ... I can't believe you aren't in horrible pain right now."

"No, not really. I drank a half a quart of Pendleton, and the nice doctor gave me some Vicodin. I'm not feeling anything right now."

Lefty limped around the ranch for a few weeks until he could take the cast off. His leg was healing nicely, so he saw no sense in wearing a walking boot. As he had planned before, he just duct taped his boot at the ankle for support and continued as if nothing had happened.

CHAPTER 3: DOWN MEXICO WAY

Gilbert Ochoa, the drug king pin who ensnared Roger Benton in his drug business, waited outside his Hacienda in Janos for his men to bring Benton to Him.

The two-man crew met Benton in Janos, blindfolded him, and proceeded to the Ochoa Ranch. Benton was not built for this kind of intrigue. He felt a fear like none he had ever felt. Although he had been an Army Ranger in the first Gulf War, he felt completely unprepared for what was to come.

As the Range Rover traveled south to Casas Grandes, his mind was working furiously for a way out of this mess. He had been summoned because of his refusal to do what Ochoa wanted. He went to Mexico not by choice, but because Ochoa had threatened his wife and daughter if he refused to come. He thought about contacting the authorities, but fear for his families safety changed his mind. Now he was headed straight into the mouth of the dragon, knowing full well that he might not make it out alive.

"Bien venidos señor Benton, Ochoa, greeted the terrified man. I trust your journey was uneventful?"

When Benton refused to answer Ochoa, one of his thugs power punched him in the gut.

"Parate, hombre, how can he speak when he can't breathe?"

"Sorry Patron."

"I will make this simple. You either keep making runs, or you will never see your wife and children again, entiendes?"

"You don't understand. I can't take the risk anymore. It's too dangerous. If I'm caught, I'll lose everything," Benton groaned.

"I don't care about you pendejo, I care about filling my orders. Maybe a few days in the hot house will help you change your mind. Get him out of here, throw him in the carcel."

By the end of the next day, Celine Benton was worried. Her husband had not called, and she did not know what had happened to him. She called everyone she knew, but they had not seen or heard from him either. Even the cattle sale staff in Roswell reported that he never made it there. Fearing the worst, she went to the bunkhouse to ask Lefty and JR for help.

"Good evening, Mrs. Benton. Sorry the place is in such a mess. Can we help you?"

"Mr. Benton said he was going to Roswell yesterday and, for sure, would be back this evening, I have not heard from him, and I am afraid something bad has happened."

"I'm sure he is alright ma'am, may have had a flat or something,"

"No, I feel it, something bad has happened. Can you please help me?"

"Ma'am, Lefty said, we know about everyone in the cattle business. I'll make a few calls and see if I can find something out."

"Thank you so much mijo, I'm truly grateful."

JR and Lefty got on the phone immediately and began making calls. After not having any luck with ranchers, Lefty began calling the family in Mexico just in case someone knew something. After a long conversation in Spanish with an uncle in Janos, Mexico, he returned and reported what he had learned.

"Not good, bro, not good at all."

"What do you mean, Lefty?"

"My uncle Genaro told me some disturbing news. He told me that Gilbert Ochoa's men met a gringo in Janos driving a blue F-350 pickup with New Mexico plates. He also said that there was a brand painted on the door … it looked like a bucket bail."

"Dang, that's Mr. Benton's truck … what in heck was he doing with Ochoa?"

"I don't know, but it can't be good."

"Does your uncle know where Ochoa lives?"

"He works on his ranch … so yeah, he does."

"Would he be willing to help us?"

"I don't know JR …. everyone is scared stupid of Ochoa."

JR and Lefty debated about telling Elise and her mother about Benton. If he was up to something no good, they sure didn't want to be the ones to narc him out. By this time, both mother and daughter were fearing the worst.

The Ochoa ranch was south of Haystack Mountain about 25 miles by horseback across the desert. If they rode flat out, they could get there in two hours. The problem was getting back across the border.

"How does this sound, pard? We take two horses apiece and ride flat out to the Ochoa ranch, change horses at the halfway point, and then go find Benton. After we find him, we will hightail it back to Janos, get his truck, and drive it back across the border."

"Sounds like a plan, but we are gonna need some fire power when we get there, most likely, and we will have to toss the guns before we get to the border crossing on the return trip."

"Toss my guns JR?"

"Why is that a problem, Lefty?"

"Well … because all I have is my Colt 1911 and a Winchester 30-30 my grandpa gave me … I would hate to lose them."

"It looks like there is no choice."

"I'm just taking the pistol, then."

After Lefty had called his uncle and told him the plan, his uncle agreed to help as best he could. He would meet them to catch the horses and make sure that the horses got back home again. They learned the ranch headquarters where Ochoa usually stayed was actually in Rancho San Basilio, which made it a lot closer. Still, it was a long ride across open desert at night.

The pair crept down to the stables and picked four of the fastest horses on the ranch. Instead of the heavy western style roping saddles, they picked a pair of old McClellan saddles like the cavalry once rode. They were light, smaller, and were no enormous loss if they couldn't bring them home. They also used bosal's instead of a bitted head stall, so the horses could function a little easier. Lefty was a certified journeyman farrier and had only days before shod these four horses, so there was no danger of a lost shoe that would slow them down.

Riding across the flat desert seems like a simple proposition however, there was soft sand and prairie dog holes that could break a horse's leg in a heartbeat. They would also have to go around Las Palmas mountain and then ride the arroyos until they got to where Benton was. No matter the potential danger, though, they had to make the attempt.

Lefty used an old horse thief trick of stuffing cotton balls in the horse's nostrils until they were out of hearing range of the ranch house. Horses get worked up when they leave their buddies, and start whinnying loudly, which would undoubtedly alert the ranch house.

"Dang JR, you don't want to put a whole bale of cotton up their noses. They still have to breathe."

"I was just making sure they had enough."

"The idea is to block off just enough air in their nostrils, so they can't inhale all at once to whinny, not suffocate them."

After they had walked a distance from the ranch house, they pulled the nose plugs out and headed into the night.

Elise Benton had seen everything. Little did Lefty, or JR know but Elise had waited for them to get a distance away from the stables and saddled two horses of her own.

"Do you hear something, JR?"

"Sounds like a couple of horses running towards us. Dang it!, that can only be Elise following us."

Sure enough, not more than a minute after they pulled up to listen, that Elise came loping towards them."

"I don't know what's going on, but if it involves my dad, then I am going to help."

"Elise, dang it, this is way too dangerous for you."

"You tell me what is going on JR Reilly, or I swear I will never speak to you again."

Reluctantly, JR explained to her what was going on, and what their plan was. Elise sobbed when she learned what had happened to her dad.

"Elise, if you really want to help, you must listen to me. The only hole in this plan is that we need to get back over the border again.

"That's the only hole?" Lefty chuckled.

"Anyway, if we don't have your dad's truck keys, we can't get back. Hopefully, he still has them on him. If he doesn't, we have another problem all together."

"I have a key to his truck right here on my key ring."

Relieved, JR reached out and took the keys from Elise. Elise grabbed his hand and said, "Please, bring my dad back ... I'm gonna call my uncle Tom. He is an officer with ICE. He will for sure help any way he can."

"Thank you ... now please, let us get on our way."

Heading due south in the darkness, it wasn't long before the boy's eyes adjusted to the dark and they could tell where they were at. Both JR and Lefty had worked cattle on this side of the border many times in the past. This was his uncle Genaro's ranch before he lost it all. Ochoa had forced him to sign over the deed to his property, and promised to pay him, but after three years, all Genaro had was a poor paying job on his own ranch. Ochoa had intimidated everyone to where they just did what he said and didn't argue; the safest way to remain breathing.

As the boys got to Las Palmas mountain, they had to slow down as they moved into the sandy bottom of the arroyo.

"You know, Lefty, even if we get Mr. Benton back, that still doesn't square things with Ochoa. The only way that Benton is going to be free of this thing is if Ochoa is arrested or killed."

"My uncle said the same thing, JR. But I don't think I'm up for a life spent in a Mexican Jail."

"Me either."

"But there are a lot of ways to bring a guy down without

killing him, JR. I think a plan is about to be born. Genaro said that Ochoa has a stash house out here somewhere."

"At the ranch?"

"Yup."

"Why didn't you say something about this before?"

"Well, you see JR, sometimes great minds like mine must work unobstructed until the light bursts forth into a great idea. Not having to listen to you talk while we had to ride at a full gallop has been like the Balm of Gilead for my brain."

"What?"

"I don't know, something my mama Reilly was reading about in the Bible ... anyway, Genaro also said that Ochoa had an escape tunnel than ran from the ranch house in San Basilio, to this concrete reinforced building a few miles away. Ochoa keeps most of his cash there. Genaro said that he was so impressed with 'El Chapo' Guzman, that he dug a tunnel in his honor.

"That was lame. Did he tell you anything else?"

"Yeah, he said that there were guards, and it was built like Fort Knox."

"Well Einstein, during this moment of great thought you were talking about, did you come up with a way to get past the guards and the other security?"

"It's obvious that you do not know the thought processes of geniuses JR. While I have no answer at this juncture, I am confident that a burst of wisdom will shortly come forth."

"Sure Pal, whatever you say."

"He mentioned that the building was on a farm where there were center pivot irrigated fields. And I remember where that is."

"So do I, Lefty, because I can see them from here.

Sure enough, as the moon came out from behind the clouds,

they could see Ochoa's farm in the distance.

"Got any ideas about where that building might be lefty?"

"If I had to guess, I would probably say to the left of us about a quarter mile, and if you would quit looking the wrong direction through the binoculars, you could see it too, dimwit."

Sure enough, at the edge of one of the cultivated fields, there was a building with a security fence around it, and only one entrance into the building.

"That looks like a bomb shelter."

"Yeah Lefty, doesn't look too promising."

As they stayed in cover, they watched as a truck came down the road and stopped at the fence gate entrance. A heavy-set man got out of the truck, walked to the gate, and just pushed it open; it wasn't even locked. When the man went through the entryway of the building, they could hear someone yelling in Spanish.

"You are supposed to be standing guard, you idiot, not drinking tequila. If I had been Mr. Ochoa … you would be dead. If you weren't my wife's favorite nephew, I would kill you myself!"

"It's boring out here Tio" the nephew whined, "No one ever comes out here. Nobody would dare try to steal from him."

"You just stay awake! And no more drinking."

The man stomped away and didn't even bother to lock the gate behind him. He got in the truck and drove back the way he came."

"I am prepared to reveal the next part of the plan, JR."

"Shut up, Lefty, we gotta go."

As JR and Lefty crept up to the gate and went inside the enclosure, the door to the building was wide open and the guard had his back to it, watching Mexican wrestling on a TV that was so small, he had to put his face a foot from the screen to see it. Lefty walked up behind him and clobbered him in the head with the butt of his pistol; the man went limp and fell to the floor in a heap.

"You know JR, there should be a manual, or a training booklet that teaches you how hard to hit a man to knock him out."

"Do you see that goose egg on his head? I think that was just right."

"If you say so, but maybe I should hit him again just to be sure?"

"Lefty, we are wasting time. Just tie him up with that extension cord and let's get out of here."

"And out of the gate comes Lefty Ortiz. Watch as he ropes the calf, then leaps off his horse, throws down the calf, and ties three legs with two wraps and a hooey. World Record time ... the crowd roars."

JR walked over to Lefty and conked him on the head with his pistol. "What the? ... dang it, that hurt!"

"If you are through, we have a rescue mission to get to. We need to put him in that closet, so no one sees him.

After hiding the guard, they discovered that to get to the tunnel, they had to descend a ladder that went down almost twenty feet. The tunnel itself was well constructed, reinforced with heavy timber at regular intervals, with lights every ten feet, and a rail system that went the entire length of it. Sitting on the rail was a battery-operated golf cart with steel train wheels to accommodate the track.

"Up for a ride Lefty?"

"You bet. Let's go."

"JR, there might be an opening or two along this tunnel. I read that narco- trafficante's build places where they store stuff along the tunnels, and where men can sleep. We best be careful."

"Where did you read that?"

"You know at Rodeo's Bar and Grill? They have stuff to read in the bathroom while you're standing there taking a whiz? I read it there."

JR just looked at Lefty and shook his head.

There were no places dug out for 'sleeping men or stuff' the entire length of the tunnel. But it was a seriously long tunnel; at least 10 miles. Up ahead, they could see where the tunnel ended, so they slowed the golf cart to a stop and walked the rest of the way with their pistols in hand. As they climbed up the ladder to the top, they found it opened into a crawl space behind a wooden planked wall. Peering through the cracks, they could see that behind the wall was a tack room.

There was a door visible from the inside but disguised on the tack room side.

"Lefty, it looks like we are in the horse barn, but someone has stacked bales of hay on the other side of this door to the tack room. I don't think it's gonna open."

"You best let me do the thinking JR, it opens inward."

Sure enough, while JR was busy pushing on the door, Lefty could see that the hinges were hung to open inside.

"I knew that, Lefty. I was just testing to see how observant you were."

"Sure Pal."

When they opened the door, there was just enough room to climb over the hay bales and into the tack room. The tack room opened into a breezeway where there were at least twenty stalls on either side.

"Lefty, I have a feeling we better check each one of these stalls. I might be wrong, but Mr. Benton could be in one of them."

The boys split up, one going to the left, the other to the right, looking in each stall. The breezeway in the horse barn was poorly lit, so it was difficult to see too far ahead. As JR got to the end of the stalls he was inspecting, he could see a man sitting in a chair in front of one of the last stalls, with a shotgun in his lap.

He looked around for Lefty, but he was nowhere to be seen. Realizing he was going to have to take out the sleeping guard himself, he crept up to him as quietly as possible to knock him out. As he raised his pistol, out of nowhere, a huge rock came flying in and hit the man squarely in the forehead.

"Just like David and Goliath," Lefty laughed.

"I swear Lefty, someday I'm gonna smother you in your sleep."

"What? Why, I just saved your life."

"No time, I'll explain later. We have to look for Benton."

JR searched the guard's pockets till he found the key to the locked stall. As he opened the door, he was surprised to find not only Mr. Benton, but Lefty's uncle Genaro as well.

"You boys are a sight for sore eyes,"

"No time to talk, Mr. Benton. We have to go."

As the boys prepared to leave, Lefty hugged his uncle and asked why he was in the stall, too.

"I was tired of Ochoa not paying me, so I confronted him. He had his men beat me and throw me in here. If you hadn't come, I'm sure he would have killed me. Thank you mijo, I owe you, my life."

"No Tio, don't say that. I'm just glad we came when we did."

We have to go. Uncle Genaro, is there a vehicle that we can

take back across the border?"

"Ochoa has a garage with two Sand Rails in it. All the guards will be drunk at this hour. If we hurry, we might get back across the border without them finding out."

The four men crept quietly to the barn, found the keys to the two Sand Rails, and started them up.

"What the heck! don't these things have mufflers?"

"Let's get out of here, drunk or not. Everyone will hear the roar of these things."

With Lefty and Genaro in one, and JR and Benton in the other, the men pointed the Sand Rails north, hoping to get back across the border before they were caught.

"Can't these things go any faster?"

"I've got it topped out now, Mr. Benton. It's as fast as she goes."

"I see motorcycle headlights behind us. They look like they are catching up."

With Lefty in the lead, and JR close behind him, the motorcycles were catching up to them fast.

Benton was keeping watch behind them when he shouted, "They are firing machine guns at us!"

No sooner had the words escaped his lips that he screamed in pain, and grabbed his right arm, a bullet had hit its mark.

"Are you ok?, how bad is it?"

"It's just a flesh wound, but we have to do something before they kill us all."

Riding the horses through the arroyos was the best way to get to Ochoa's ranch, but there was no way that these Sand Rails would fit down those narrow gullies. To make matters worse, the terrain at Las Palmas mountain got rougher than a cob. It would make traveling in these glorified dune buggies almost impossible. Suddenly, JR had an idea. Pushing his gas pedal to the floor, he pulled alongside Lefty and yelled, "Go to where we left the horses!"

Lefty gave a thumbs up in response.

JR remembered that they had hobbled all four of the horses, so they wouldn't wander too far. They pushed the Sand Rails hard until they had a little breathing room, then stopped in front of the same arroyo from where they had entered the Ochoa farm from. Stopping the engines, they made a mad dash up the ravine to the little watering hole where the horses were calmly waiting.

"Me and Lefty will fire a few rounds at those guys shooting at us. You two get the horses ready. We are going to have to split up, so when we are ready, Mr. Benton, you go Northeast to Haystack mountain, Genaro, you go at least a mile east of him and then North to the border. JR and I are going to get spotted by the Aerostat balloons and get some help. Elise told us that your brother was with ICE? she was going to contact him so we could get some help."

"Does Elise know what's going on?" Benton asked grimly.

"No, because we weren't sure what was going on, either. And if your wife knows anything, it didn't come from us."

"I appreciate it, fellers."

JR and Lefty went to the top of a ledge high above the ravine and waited for the motorcycle riders to come down the arroyo, but they never came. The three motorcycles that were chasing them turned around and went back.

As the pair mounted the last two horses and headed them to the U.S. border, it became clear why the motorcycles had bugged out. Right on the border of the U.S. and Mexico, two Black Hawk helicopters hovered in the dark. Ochoa's men undoubtedly had been monitoring radio transmissions and learned that two Black Hawk's had been dispatched to their area.

"Are they gonna take my pistol, JR?"

"Do you know what the penalty for carrying a firearm in Mexico is? I'll buy you another pistol if you quit whining. Throw it away before you go to jail."

Well, Mr. Benton came clean with his wife, and she forgave him, but the U.S. government didn't. He went to trial and got a few month's probation but didn't lose his ranch.

Benton's brother Tom caught two of Ochoa's gunmen red handed in Columbus, New Mexico, trying to assassinate the town mayor. They rolled over on Ochoa, and he was extradited to the United States, sentenced to life in prison at La Tuna Federal Penitentiary, and was dead within a month at the hand of a person, or persons unknown.

As for Elise and JR, she was incredibly grateful to him for saving her dad's life single-handedly, with the slight help of Lefty, though he wasn't a major contributor.

When Elise found out the true story, she slapped JR and never wanted to see him again, which was all right with Mr. Benton, except he was sad to lose his top hands.

Lefty got his pistol back, because instead of throwing it away, he hid it in the cavity of a rock with an arrow pointing to it. Uncle Genaro retrieved it for him; after all, it was Genaro's father who had given Lefty the pistol. And, oh yeah; Uncle Genaro got his ranch back, complete with a stash house full of cash.

CHAPTER 4: THE CASE OF THE SNEAKY HORSE THIEF.

After JR's unfortunate incident with Elise, the boys figured it was time to move on. The winter was over anyway, so they headed north to greener pastures.

Greener pastures, for them, meant the bright lights of Las Vegas. Not the Nevada one, but the one north of Santa Fe.

Whenever things got slow, they always knew that they could find work at the Bell ranch down in La Cinta canyon.

They liked to spend a few days in Las Vegas to visit some ranchers in Watrous, and up towards Wagon Mound and Roy, just to be friendly. And if they had a few horses for them to shoe, so much the better.

One of their customers was a professional roper who lived in Roy, New Mexico. Oscar Martinez was so good at roping that he had a major lariat rope company as a sponsor.

"JR, you want to go see if Oscar has some horses to shoe?"

"Lefty, your memory is about as long as your tallywacker; don't you remember him trying to pay us in used ropes?"

"I know, but it was our fault that we didn't capitalize on making those rope pots out of them."

"Again, don't you remember buying the glue gun and trying to make pots and vases out of those ropes in the Motel 6 room in

Socorro?"

"I remember we had a few problems turning them into pots."

"The problem was Oscar is a heeler, and he uses extra hard lay ropes. They are so stiff they call them cables!"

"Man! the motel manager was hopping mad, when one of those pots he bought off of us suddenly un-coiled and busted out the windows in the motel office," Lefty was laughing so hard he coughed.

JR began laughing uncontrollably in response, "Bryan Williams says they have our picture up in the lobby on a sort of wanted poster... it says wanted dead or alive!"

"Whew, that was funny JR. One of these days, we are gonna have to grow up." JR and Lefty looked at each other and said, "Nah."

Stopping in the local feed store, Lefty went to talk to the manager while JR looked at the bulletin board.

Wanted: good horse shoer to shoe six head of horses. Horses have been handled and will stand for trimming but have never been shod. Will pay top dollar. Call (505) 555-2256

"Lefty, look at this!"

"That looks right up our alley, don't it?"

"Let's call them."

"Hello?"

"Yes sir, my name is JR Reilly. Me and my partner are Certified Journeymen Farriers, and we noticed your ad in the feed store."

"Yes, that's right."

"We were wondering if the horses still needed shoeing. If so, we would like the job."

"I'm not gonna lie to you son, they are a handful, but if you're experienced, they shouldn't be a problem. What do you charge?"

"85 dollars per head."

"When can you do them?"

"We can do them today. All we need is the directions."

"If you take the first Las Vegas exit going north from Santa Fe, and go east about one mile, you will come to a cattle guard. Turn right at the cattle guard and drive south until you come to a big pasture with an old red box car outside the fence that we use to store grain and such . There are six bay horses there in that pasture. Shoe them all around, and I'll be in town tomorrow to pay you."

"Sounds like a deal. Thank you, sir."

"Ok son, we just made $510 dollars. We need to get some shoes and nails."

Most light horses wear size '0' shoes in the front, and '00' in the back. Rarely do you see a quarter horse that needs a shoe bigger than a '1' in the front, and '0' in the back.

JR gets the Saint Croix shoes that have the pre-shaped hinds, at least three pairs of aughts, and three pairs of double aughts. We also will need a three pair of aught and three pairs of number 1 front shoes. They will save us some time. Also get Delta #5 City Head Slim Nails, the 500 count."

"Why get the big box?"

"Because we won't be near any place to buy nails if we go to the Bell Ranch, and all I have are those crappy Mustad nails in my shoeing box."

"Fair enough."

Following the instructions that the man gave them, they soon came upon the red box car and the fenced in pasture.

Centered on the boxcar, there was a dividing fence that cut the big pasture in two.

Just as the horse's owner said, there were six heads of bay horses in one pen. Catching two of the horses, Lefty and JR had them both shod in less than forty minutes. Within three hours, they had all six horses beautifully shod.

"JR, didn't that guy say that these horses were a handful?"

"Yeah, but because of our skill level, they didn't stand a chance."

Lefty just shrugged his shoulders and put his shoeing tools up. Eager to get paid and on down the road, they took their bill to the feed store and called the owner.

"Well, that was quick, did they give you any trouble?"

"No sir, they were perfect gentlemen," JR said boastfully

"You mean perfect ladies, don't you? There were six bay mares in the pen."

At this point, JR was panicking. He knew that he and Lefty had shod six head of geldings.

"Could you hold for a minute, sir?"

JR started quizzing Lefty about the horses.

"Lefty, please tell me that those horses we just shod were mares?"

"Nope ... six head of geldings. Why?"

"Pardon me sir, I'm getting another call, and I'll need to take it. Can I call you back?"

"Dad gummit Lefty! we shod the wrong horses"

By the time that the boys made it back to the pasture where they had shod the horses, it was feeding time. Sure enough, in the one pasture were six head of freshly shod bay geldings, and right next door, six head of unshod bay mares that had come up from the far end of the pasture where you couldn't see them.

JR threw his hat on the ground and began kicking and punching the sides of the red box car. Lefty just watched and laughed uncontrollably.

"What the heck are you laughing for?"

"I'm laughing because we don't have any shoes left to do the horses we were supposed to do, and no money to buy more. Our only option is to jerk the shoes off the geldings and shoe the mares with them."

And so, they did.

The next day, the horse owner came out and inspected the shoeing job the boys had done and was quite impressed.

"You guys did a great job. In a few weeks, I'll have you come and shoe those six head of geldings in the other pasture. I was gonna have you trim them, but it doesn't look like they need it."

Lefty was drinking a soda pop when the horse owner made the comment, and blew soda pop out of his nose, laughing. JR just looked straight ahead and never flinched.

With 500 dollars of hard-earned money in their pockets, less the cost of replenishing their shoe supply, the boys headed to Trementina, a little town east of Las Vegas. About halfway through their trip, there was a pickup truck with a 10 horse horse trailer broke down on the side of the road. JR slowed the truck down and Lefty hollered out the window.

"Need any help?"

"Looks like my radiator hose gave out. Have a spare?"

Looking up from under the hood, a grizzled old man with a

week's growth of beard stood up to talk to the boys. His straw cowboy hat was so beat up, the brim was torn away from the crown in the front. The pickup he drove had seen its better days, but the trailer appeared brand new, or at least just a few months old.

"No, we don't, but we could take you back to Vegas to get one at the Auto Parts store."

"I've got a trailer full of horses. I can't leave them."

"Well, we could head back to Vegas and bring you one? We would have to be repaid, though. We aren't exactly flush."

"I would appreciate it. I can pay you," the man said as he pulled out a roll of hundred-dollar bills as big around as a coke can from his pocket.

Lefty got out of the truck to help the man remove the radiator hose from the truck motor. Out of curiosity, JR went to the horse trailer and admired the ten head of horses the man had in there.

"Man, those are some nice ponies." The man didn't answer.

"I said those are some nice horse's sir, you raise them yourself?"

Again, the man didn't answer, so JR just dropped it. Soon the pair had the hose off the motor and were headed back to Vegas to buy the old man a new one. JR cringed when he heard the price, but he paid it and headed back down to where the old man and the trailer were on the side of the road. As they approached, they were surprised to see two State Police units, a County Mounty, and the Cattle Inspector with lights flashing, surrounding the truck and trailer. JR slowed the truck to a stop as one of the State Troopers flagged him down.

"I need to check your license and registration."

"Sure Officer, what's going down?"

"Is that you JR?"

"In the flesh, you remember Lefty, don't you?"

"I sure do. I thought you two would be in prison by now."

"We are just too tricky, Charlie; they can't catch us."

Charlie Hastings was a relative of JR's some way, though no one was sure how. He was about the same age and had gone to college with he and Lefty. Charlie was a Criminal Science major; looked like he fulfilled his dream of being a cop.

"So, Charlie, what's going on?"

"This trailer was stolen. It belongs to a racehorse ranch down in Belen."

"What happened to the horses?"

"What horses JR? he just stole the trailer as far as we could tell."

"Listen Charlie, I'll be straight with you, we are on our way back from Vegas where we bought an old man a radiator hose for that old pickup, and when we left, he had a ten head of some pretty nice ponies in the trailer."

Charlie called the Cattle Inspector over and told him what JR had said.

"Are you sure about the horses? We don't have a report about stolen horses."

"Absolutely sure. I even asked where he got them, but he wouldn't answer, so I quit asking."

"Can you describe him?"

"He looked to be in his late 70's, 5' 8", skinny as a rail, long gray hair, weeks' worth of beard, wearing an old straw hat that had seen its better days."

"This is real important son, are you sure your description is accurate?"

"Yes sir," both boys said in unison.

The Cattle Inspector pulled Charlie over to the front of JR and Lefty's pickup and began moving his hands wildly. He was so animated that Lefty chuckled.

"We are gonna need for you to make a formal statement, JR."

"Sure Charlie, can I ask why?"

"Well, there are no hoofprints around the trailer that would show someone took the horses, and no fresh manure in the trailer to say they were ever there. What's more, that man you described is old man Whitaker."

"We bought him a radiator hose for his truck Charlie, we know we saw him."

"Did you say you helped take the hose off?"

"Yes, sir."

"Hose is on the pickup motor, hasn't been removed."

"This is getting weird," Lefty said as a shiver went down his spine.

So, once again, JR and Lefty traveled the road back to Las Vegas, and on to the State Police headquarters to make a statement about the old man.

"Charlie, I got a pretty good look at those horses. They all had run down bandages on their hind legs, manes were pulled for the track, and they were shod with Race Plates."

The Cattle Inspector had a doubtful look on his face. "You saw all that from looking through the slats of the trailer?"

Charlie came to JR's defense, "trust me, if JR said he saw it, he saw it; these boys are two of the best horse shoers in the country."

The Cattle Inspector was a short, fat man, with an enormous belly, who always chewed a cigar that he kept in the corner of his mouth.

"Does that Inspector remind you of someone?"

Lefty laughed, "Yeah .... Boss Hogg from the Dukes of Hazard."

"Why do you think he got so freaked out over your description of that old man JR?"

"I don't know, but I'm gonna corner Charlie and ask."

JR and Lefty caught Charlie outside the State Police headquarters and quizzed him about "Boss Hogg". Come to find out, Old man Whitaker had been stealing horses in New Mexico and hauling them to Texas and beyond, and no one could ever catch him.

Tom Bleeker, the Cattle inspector, tried for years to run him down, but he never could. Bleeker became a joke, and a by word, for someone who was completely incompetent. Folks in law enforcement would say that they had been "Bleekered" when referring to the one who got away.

As fate would have it, Whitaker was arrested in Deaf Smith County, Texas, after a traffic stop for a busted headlight. When the Deaf Smith Sheriff discovered who he was, they tried him for horse theft, and he got two years in the Deaf Smith County jail; he died in jail under mysterious circumstances.

Bleeker had tried unsuccessfully to have him brought back to New Mexico, but no dice. The Sheriff in Texas is the highest law enforcement entity in the state; they don't answer to anybody for county business.

After getting their money back from the Auto Parts store, JR and Lefty headed back towards Trementina, and then the Bell ranch. When they got where they stopped for the old man, both the truck and trailer were gone; no doubt impounded by the

State Police.

Lefty let's stop here for a minute. I want to look around where that trailer was."

As the two boys got out to look around, sure enough, there were no hoof prints anywhere to show a horse had been there. There was a shallow sandy bottomed arroyo that went south from the road as far as they could see.

"I'm going up this arroyo a way. I have a hunch what went down here."

"What do you mean, JR?"

"The Oldest horse thief trick in the book. Tie a rope to the last horse's tail attached to a mesquite bush, tie the rest of the horses' head to tail, pony them in a straight line, and let the mesquite bush cover your tracks. I didn't notice it before, but look, there was a good-sized mesquite bush here that somebody cut off at ground level."

Lefty started laughing.

"What are you laughing at, numbskull?"

"I was just remembering the last time we tied a mesquite bush to a live animal."

JR started laughing too, "Ole' Blue Jay sure reacted to a burning bush differently than Moses did."

Walking up the sandy arroyo almost half a mile, there were suddenly horse tracks, and a pile of manure dumped unceremoniously on top of a cactus.

"You know what JR, that old boy came prepared. Those horses had diapers on just like those on 16th street in Denver have. That's why the trailer was clean."

Sure enough, under the pile of manure were some plastic 'horse diapers'. It used to not matter about leaving a pile of manure here and there on the road. Now, horses traveled with diapers on so that the manure wouldn't fall through the cracks and hit an unsuspecting motorist traveling behind the trailer.

"I wish we had time. I would like to follow this out to see where he took the horses."

"JR, let's get to Trementina and see if old Don Pablo will loan us a four-wheeler, if he has gotten over you jilting his granddaughter that is."

"That was three years ago. Surely, he can't hold a grudge that long. Besides, she got married and is gonna have a baby pretty soon. That is yesterday's news."

Yesterday's news to everyone except Don Pablo. He would loan Lefty the use of a Four-Wheeler, but he didn't want JR to drive it, only Lefty. He also wanted JR to apologize to his granddaughter on his knees while Don Pablo watched, which he did... it was hilarious.

"Carmen, please forgive me for embarrassing you..."

"And humiliating her!" Don Pablo coached.

"And humiliating you..."

"And for making her cry for days!"

"And for making you cry for days."

"I wish I could just kill myself for hurting her."

"I wish I ... whoa, what?"

"You heard me! Just say it or no Four-Wheeler."

"I wish I could just kill myself for hurting you."

Carmen stood beside her grandfather and tried to stifle a laugh. "It's ok JR, I was over you after the first week."

Lefty could not quit laughing. His jaw ached from laughing so much. They loaded the Four-Wheeler on the back of the pickup and headed to where the truck and trailer were.

"I swear Lefty, if you ever tell anyone about that, I will skin you alive."

Laughing hysterically, Lefty blurted out, "Carmen recorded the whole thing on her iPhone! It's probably on Instagram now, as we speak!"

JR's face turned red, and his ears felt like they were burning. He would never live this down.

The pair followed hoof prints almost five miles on the four-wheeler until the arroyo widened into a deep gorge, with walls at least 100 feet high on two sides.

"This would be a dangerous place to get stuck at in a rainstorm JR, no way to get out."

"I was just thinking that. Seems like a weird place to be taking horses. "

Driving through a narrow corridor just wide enough for the four-wheeler to pass through, the arroyo opened up into a round box canyon that was probably hidden until you were right up to the edge.

"You two hold it right there," a voice called out.

Looking around, the two saw that same old man who had been broken down on the side of the road, but this time he was holding a Winchester 30-30 on them.

"Don't shoot Mr. Whitaker, we aren't here for trouble."

"Who told you my name?" the old man demanded.

"The Cattle Inspector, Tom Bleeker."

"Get off that contraption and walk toward me ... no tricks! I will shoot you."

Lefty killed the engine on the four-wheeler and the pair

walked with their hands up over to Whitaker.

Moving behind the two boys, Whitaker told them to keep walking.

Behind a row of big mesquite bushes was a hidden entrance to a cave that had to be thirty feet across and thirty feet high. The cave was formed from limestone, and there was a stream of clear water running through it. About one hundred feet inside the cave was a set of corrals, and inside the corrals were not only the ten head of race colts JR saw in the trailer, but about twenty head more. There also was a haystack with at least one 1000 bales of timothy hay, and a couple of pallets of bagged whole oats.

"I don't know how you found me, but it puts me in a predicament."

"We don't want trouble Mr., If you let us go, we won't tell anyone about this place."

"I want to know how you found me," Whitaker demanded once again.

"You used an old horse thief trick. You ponied the horses tied head to tail, and on last horse you attached a mesquite bush ."

"I have used that trick over the years a hundred times. No one ever figured it out," the old man chuckled.

"I want to know how you got that hay in here," Lefty asked.

"So, you see back in the cave where there is light shining down from the top. It's an opening about 20 feet round. I have kind of an 'A'-frame hoist topside, and a pallet attached to a heavy cable that will hold about 30 bales of hay. I bolted the cable to the front of my truck with a clevis, then backed up till the load cleared the lip of the hole, drove forward lowering the load, crawled down and unloaded the hay, and kept doing it till I finished."

"By yourself?"

"All by myself, took a while."

"I have another question, Mr. Whitaker. Those colts you ponied here. How did you get them to cooperate? JR and I have trained pack horses, but it takes a while to make them behave without kicking each other's heads off when you tie them head to tail. If you took these horses green from the Belen ranch, that should have been quite a rodeo."

"I really can't talk about that, son. Though I will tell you that there are some marvelous pharmaceuticals coming out of Mexico that do some amazing things."

"Mr. Whitaker, everybody thinks you died in the Deaf Smith County jail several years ago."

Whitaker chuckled, "My cousin is the Sheriff. I spent a year at his house, then we pretended I died so I could come back to New Mexico."

"It's none of my business but, are all those horses stolen?"

"I stole them for sure. But it's not what you think. You said you met Bleeker, right?"

Both boys nodded yes.

"That sorry so and so is crookeder than a dog's hind leg. I never stole a single head, but he discovered I found out about his little scam, and so he tried to paint me as a horse thief, and got it done, too."

"Well, we didn't like him much, did we Lefty?"

"Nope."

"So, what was this scam?"

"There were two parts; for years, maybe decades, Bleeker had been taking mongrel horses that were put together pretty well and fixing them up with phony papers to make them look like they were hot-blooded racehorses. He would then make a killing on them at sale."

"What's the second part?"

"Collecting semen from common stud horses and bootlegging it to breeders as top bloodline breeding stock. I drew blood on all of those horses back there and sent it off for DNA testing. Not a one of them has a single drop of top one hundred performance horse blood in their veins."

"Let me guess, that ranch in Belen. They are conspiring with Bleeker?"

"You got it. They are thick as thieves, but they aren't the only ones. There are a few in Oklahoma, Arizona, and Colorado. Bleeker would inspect the horses, falsify a Coggins test, and ship them out of state. A Coggins is a blood test that detects antibodies to the disease Equine Infectious Anemia; that is highly contagious. They couldn't take a chance that there might be random DNA test, so they just doctored the results to show negative Coggins.

"Me and Lefty have been on horse ranches where there was an outbreak of Infectious anemia, it ain't pretty."

"I also found out that he had imported at least fifty common old Mexican mares, and artificially inseminated them with any halfway decent stud horse he could find. These horses are the second crop of colts from those mares. Do you see the sorrel colt with the blaze, and the red roan filly? Their papers say they are by Flashing Eagle. He is a copper red sorrel horse with a blaze. They would shop around their herd for a colt that had similar color and markings, and POOF, they are sired by an All-American

Futurity winner."

"It was lucky we came by instead of someone else. Me and JR will help you Mr. Whitaker."

"I can't ask you to do that. I am a felon. You would be aiding and abetting."

"Well, as it so happens, JR and I haven't been in trouble for a while. We are behind in our quota."

"Lefty and I know everybody who owns a horse from Raton to Sunland Park. If you could document for us which bloodline has been forged, and which frozen semen is bogus, we can pass the word to every horse owner we know. They know which horses they bought, and what semen they were supposed to buy. I'll bet that in a no time, Bleeker and his cronies will look out from behind bars."

And that's exactly what they did. Within a few weeks, all the horse owners who had been swindled by Bleeker and company were calling for heads to roll. The Quarter horse governing body, realizing there was a hole in their registration program, took steps to make DNA testing mandatory, before a horse could be registered to a particular sire or dam. The test had to be performed by a certified laboratory, and the chain of custody maintained until the results were recorded.

Mr. Whitaker was exonerated from charges of horse thieving; but refused to move out of his cave. There are rumors he was giving tours of his cave for ten bucks a head; but you know how rumors get started.

As for Bleeker ... they sent him to Santa Fe Penitentiary; where he is now called Bubba and is Big Leroy's favorite.

The ranch in Belen was sued by everybody and anybody until

they filed for bankruptcy protection. But bankruptcy protection would not get them out of the fix they were in south of the border, because a Mexican drug Cartel owned 25 bogus colts.

And JR and Lefty? they found a coke can sized roll of 100-dollar bills in their truck box ... courtesy of Mr. Whitaker.

Unfortunately, Don Pablo has still not changed his opinion of JR.

CHAPTER 5: NO GOOD DEED GOES UNPUNISHED

With more cash money than they have ever had before, JR and Lefty went looking for investment opportunities.

"Lefty, how much did you say was in that roll of money?"

"How much WAS there, or how much IS there?"

"Why do I care how much there was?"

"Because knowing how much there was will prevent you from spending more of how much there is."

"Ok, dimwit, how much was there?"

"25 thousand dollars"

"And how much left?"

"10 thousand dollars."

"What!!, how did we blow 15 thousand dollars in seven days?"

"Well, assuming that question was not rhetorical, you're wearing 300 dollars on your head, another 250 on your feet, and in between your hat and your boots you bought 500 worth of jeans and shirts... and I did the same."

"That's only 22 hundred dollars. Where is the rest?"

"Well, since you asked, we usually sleep in the pickup and shower in a truck stop. We spent three nights in the Holiday Inn Express in Las Vegas ... at two hundred bucks per night. Then we ate three meals a day. We bought new tires for the truck, got the truck serviced, and so here we are with ten thousand dollars left over. Oh yeah, I forgot to say, I put 10 thousand in the savings account ... can't spend it if you don't have it on you."

"I'm really reluctant to say this to you because it will probably go to your head but, that was smart thinking."

"My mind is like a steel trap,"

"More like a leaky bucket, Lefty."

"Well, yours is like, uhhh...."

"Give it up, Lefty, your way over your head. Sarcasm must be snappy." JR snaps his fingers in front of Lefty's nose.

"You best get your fingers out of my face before you lose them."

"Just making a point, pard."

"The only point I see is the point on top of your head."

"See, that's much better. It was snappy. Actually Lefty, the word 'sarcasm' is Latin for snappy."

"You know what JR; of all the dumb things you have said in your life; that was by far the dumbest."

"Which part?"

"Oh My Gosh! Never mind! I'm gonna take a nap."

Headed south on I-25, JR stayed quiet for about thirty minutes and then decided Lefty had enough nap.

"I think we ought to go to Sunland Park."

"For what?" Lefty mumbled, still half asleep.

"With our horse knowledge, we could clean up at the track."

"JR, the only thing we will clean up is the parking lot when we are too broke to even buy gas."

"You lack faith, sir."

"Alright, I'll tell you what, we'll go to Sunland Park, but we only wager 500 dollars, no more, when it's gone, we are gone too; deal?"

"Ok, it's a deal."

JR headed the truck south to Sunland Park Racetrack with dollar signs in his eyes. Lefty just sat in the passenger's seat with his hat cocked over his eyes, trying to figure out how he was going to stop JR from losing their money.

This wasn't the first idea JR ever had that involved horses and wagering. A few years ago, he had taken their hard-earned money and invested in a racehorse named 'Fidel's Cubano'. He was completely convinced that this horse was a winner. The problem was the man he bought the horse from didn't own the horse. And to make matters worse, the actual owner was a drug runner from Mexico who looked pretty dimly on people taking his property. Fortunately, Lefty's dad convinced the man it was an honest mistake and to let it drop … Tomas Ortiz was a scary man when his family was threatened.

"Lefty, get the phone, it's mom."

"Which mom?"

"Mom Ortiz."

"Hi mom, what's up?"

"Lefty, is JR with you?"

"Yes, he is driving, though."

"Put the phone on speaker."

Putting the phone on speaker, the boys sensed a bit of tension in the air, because their mothers rarely called them unless it was an emergency.

"JR this is your mom. I need for you and Lefty to head over to Hatch as soon as you can … where are you?"

"We are in between Socorro and T or C mom, is there a problem? Lefty and I were heading to Sunland Park."

Mom Ortiz spoke up. "You boys are NOT going to Sunland Park because I know you two. You will bet on those horses again."

Lefty and JR looked at each other and grimaced. They knew better than to lie about it, so they just redirected the attention.

"What's going on in Hatch, mom?"

"Do you remember Allan Taylor?"

"Sure, we worked with him on the Cluff's ranch in Upham. What's going on?"

"His wife called papa Tomas and said that Allan had been out gathering cows, and he never came back. Your dad's want you to saddle up and look for them."

"Mom, isn't that the mounted patrols job?"

"They are busy rescuing people from that fire up in the Santa Fe Forest. They have no one to help. I will tell your dad's that you will be here within the hour, right?"

"Yes ma'am. We will see you in an hour."

Lefty and JR's fathers had been close friends since they were toddlers, and so had their mothers. JR's mother had been adopted by Lefty's grandparents when she was a newborn; Jr and Lefty's moms had grown up as sisters. All their lives, JR addressed Lefty's parents as Mama Ortiz, and Papa Ortiz; and Lefty had done the same with JR's parents. It may have sounded great on paper to have two sets of parents, but the reality was much different. When they got into trouble, they could expect punishment from all four.

"Dad gummit Lefty, I really wanted to go to the track."

"You can scratch that off your list; Mama Ortiz has spoken."

"Well, let's get over there and see if we can find Allen. He might just be hiding out from his wife … she is meaner than a bagful of rattlesnakes."

"JR, do you remember when she hit him in the head with the frying pan? Papa Ortiz said you could see who manufactured the pan because the logo was imprinted on his bald head."

They both started laughing.

"We need to stop in Truth or Consequences for fuel. I'll stop at the Chevron; they are usually cheaper.

I'm hungry. What do you say we get some lunch at that steak house?" JR said as his stomach audibly grumbled.

"Works for me."

After fueling up, the boys crossed the street and went into the steak house. As usual, there was a girl working there that JR had offended.

"JR, look, isn't that Lucy Myers?"

"Dang it, yep it is. I hope she doesn't spit in our food."

"I better not get the treatment because I run with you. I had nothing to do with you breaking her heart."

"Guilty by association pard. We should go somewhere else; I see them talking and pointing their fingers."

"I'm not going anywhere. I came here to eat, and that's what I'm gonna do."

In just a few minutes, another server came to take their order.

"I guess you can see that you aren't too popular here."

"My money is as good as the next man. If you have something to say, say it."

"Not me, I couldn't care less. But do you see that big guy? The short-order cook? he's

Lucy's brother."

"What are you sayin'? Is he gonna spit in my food?"

"You should be so lucky. He wants to take your head off."

"You tell him we will meet him out back in five minutes and tell him to make sure his insurance is paid up; he is gonna need it."

The server hurried back to the kitchen and told Lucy's brother what had been said, pretty soon she returned.

"He said he would meet you out back, but not the other guy," pointing to Lefty.

"Works for me, but who is gonna cook our steaks when I knock the cook out?" JR.

said casually.

"I will. I'm a better cook than he is. You sure seem confident."

Lefty spoke up. "I want the chicken fried steak, mashed potatoes and gravy, and a large Coke."

"I'll have the same," JR chimed in. "I'll be right back."

Lefty watched as the cook tore his apron off and stomped out the back door. JR walked out behind him. Within a few minutes JR came back to the table with a bruised right hand ... the cook didn't come back. The server came with their order and quickly left again.

"So, let's hear the re-ride story."

"Nothing much to tell Lefty. I walked outside, the guy came barreling at me like was gonna tackle me, but I caught him right under the chin with my knee; he went down on all fours, and then I punched him in the temple ... that was it.

JR could see Lucy crying, probably because she got her brother hurt. The fact of the matter was, JR had done nothing to Lucy Myers. He had met her at a dance, they danced all night, and then JR went home. A few weeks later, JR started running in to her in the oddest places; the grocery store, gas station, you name it, she was there. I suppose something like that was possible, but Lucy lived a hundred miles away in T or C. Finally, JR figured out that she was stalking him and told her she needed to back off. Of course, it hurt her feelings, but all they did was dance together, not like he proposed or somethin'.

As they were finishing their meal, a man came through the door with a pretty girl on his arm.

"Lefty, look! That's Allan Taylor; and that ain't his wife."

"What the heck? What do we do now?"

"Well, he sure ain't missing, and he doesn't look dead. Maybe we should go say hi?"

Lefty and JR walked over to the booth where Allan and the new girl were sitting. "Hey Allan, how's it going?" Lefty asked.

"I'm sorry, you must have me confused with someone else. My name is Craig Tolliver."

JR looked at Lefty, Lefty looked at JR, and then both of them grabbed Allan by the arm and escorted him into the parking lot, much to the alarm of the woman he was with.

"Alright, you come clean, Allan, because we are on our way to Hatch, where a posse is being formed to find your body, or at least to rescue you if you're hurt. Spill it!"

Looking for a moment like he was going to deny his identity, Allan finally took a breath, shook his head, and confessed.

"I didn't mean to cause any trouble. I just figured if it looked like I had gotten bucked off and died in a ravine somewhere, they would eventually quit looking."

"Let me give you a tip about disappearing," Lefty said, poking Allan in the chest with his finger. "You leave the country entirely.

You don't find a girlfriend less than fifty miles from where you started."

"You guys aren't gonna turn me in, are you?"

"My dad has already organized a search party. We were supposed to be there already. I don't see there is much we can do."

"Please fellers, I'm begging you, you know my wife. I can't live like that anymore; she is killing me."

"Give me and Lefty a minute to discuss this, Allan."

JR and Lefty walked out of earshot range and began discussing the problem.

"We have to let papa Ortiz know Lefty. If we don't, we will have an entirely different problem on our hands."

"We definitely don't want to get on his wrong side, but what do we do?"

"Let's call him. Tell him the truth and let him tell us what to do."

Lefty dialed his dad's number and when he answered, began reciting the events that had taken place. After a few minutes Lefty began saying, "yes sir … ok sir,… right away sir", then ended the call.

Lefty looked at JR with a 'just shoot me now' face,

"He told me we are to take Allan back to where they found his horse, knock him out with a rock so it looks like he got bucked off and hit his head, and then make like we found him."

"He ain't gonna go for that, Lefty."

"Dad said that if he refused, that we were to detain him and wait for the State Police to come get him."

"That might convince him."

"He also went on a tirade about how Allan should have been

man enough to confront his wife, instead of taking the chicken way out."

"Well, that's true. He needs to step up."

The boys went back to Allan and told him what was supposed to happen. Allan began waving his hands wildly, pulling his hair that existed only on the sides of his head and not the top, then fell down to his knees as though he were begging, but something was wrong.

"JR, I think he is having a heart attack or something."

"Do you know CPR Lefty?"

"I don't, but even if I did, I'm not kissing him back to life."

"Better call an ambulance then, 'cause I ain't either."

Within minutes, an ambulance came to take the patient to the hospital, but it looked to the boys like he was dead. The girl Allan was with never even came outside to see what was going on. When she thought no one was looking, she snuck out the front door of the restaurant and got into a waiting car that had just arrived.

Well, Allan didn't die, but he was none too happy about going back to his wife. When the boys went to visit him in the hospital, he hurled some pretty rough swear words at them; telling them they should have let him die. Allan's wife believed the boys had found her husband knocked out somewhere close to Engle; they didn't correct her. Papa Ortiz agreed with Allan that they should have let him die, but he said it with a twinkle in his eye.

As for Mama Reilly and Mama Ortiz? They cooked the boys an enormous meal of their favorite foods because they were heroes … once again, neither JR nor Lefty bothering to correct the misinformation.

CHAPTER 6:
GENTLE GIANTS,
GIANT FEED BILL

The boys received a call from a horse owner who needed ten head of horses shod, but couldn't afford to pay for it. In exchange for shoeing their light horses, they would trade them a team of Belgian draft horses, complete with harness.

"What do you think, JR?"

"I've always wanted to own a pair of draft horses, Lefty. Driving that team on 16th Street in Denver was a blast."

"It was a blast until you ran over that poor Chinese guy because you were staring at those Swedish girls."

"That was an honest mistake. It could have happened to anyone."

"Well, I don't know how to say stupid in Chinese, but I'm sure it was somewhere in that tidal wave of words he directed your way."

"Speaking of not knowing how to speak Chinese, you made it worse, Lefty. It didn't help the man's mood any by saying, "Velly Solly Tanaka san, and definitely not; domo arigato Mr. Roboto."

"At least I wasn't moving my hands like the karate kid and screaming wax on! wax off! at the top of my lungs when he attacked the carriage with his cane."

By this time, both boys were laughing hysterically at the

rehashed memory.

"Shall we at least go look at those horses?" JR asked, drying the laugh tears from his eyes.

"Never hurts to look JR. Where was he calling from?"

"Dang, the other side of Lordsburg, at Steins, almost on the Arizona border."

That's a long way to go for a free shoeing job."

"Well, we'll look at it like an investment. We can go to old Mesilla and give carriage rides on the weekends for five dollars a pop."

"Ok, but if we see Swedish Girls and a Chinese man ... we cut our losses and go home."

Steins is a ghost town in Hidalgo County, New Mexico. It was originally called Stein's Pass after the nearby pass through the Peloncillo Mountains on the border of Arizona. Both Lefty and JR had seen the sign for Steins many times before, but never had enough interest in a ramshackle ghost town to stop. When they arrived, a kindly older gentleman and his wife came out to greet them.

"I'm Clyde Samson. This is my wife Giselle."

"Pleasure to meet the both of you. I'm JR Reilly, and this is Lefty Ortiz. He doesn't talk much, but I bring him along because I feel sorry for him."

"Nice to meet both of you, and as you may have already surmised, JR here is mentally challenged, and I am court ordered to make sure he stays out of trouble."

Both Clyde and Giselle were laughing as the two cowboys hacked on each other. "We appreciate the good laugh; seems like ages since we had anything to laugh about.

"Sorry to hear that. How did you end up in this part of the world?"

"We took my retirement money, and on a lark, had a stagecoach built, bought a team of draft horses, and ten other light horses. We came out here from the Ohio Valley to make a living giving stagecoach and horseback rides up the old Butterfield Stage line, which would have worked too, but I found out I had a bum ticker, and I can't walk, much less work anymore."

"How can we help you?

"The problem is, I need all the horses shod, but we are flat broke. What I had in mind was to trade you this team of Belgian geldings with all the harness for $ 2,500."

"Well, we can give you a five-dollar discount and charge $80 per head. Ten head would be $800 per trip, times three trips would put us right at $2,400. Figuring six weeks between shoeing's, it will probably take 18 weeks to get square with you. If you will allow us the $100 leeway, I think we have a deal."

"Fine by me. We wouldn't mind if you took the team of Belgians today. You could borrow the trailer and bring it back on the next trip."

"That's pretty generous of you, Mr. Samson, not knowing us from Adam and all."

"I am a former FBI Agent Lefty. I still have some connections and I had you checked out; no offense."

The boys just looked at each other and laughed. While their exploits were sure enough wild and wooly, they were harmless. What Mr. Samson found out, and what mattered most to him, was that these two boys were the best horsemen in three states and two countries; anything else was just hearsay.

The boys went to work shoeing the ten head, and in a little over five hours, had the job done. Clyde and Giselle had excused themselves earlier because Clyde had a doctor's appointment in Lordsburg. Before he left, he pointed the trailer out to them they would use to haul the Belgians.

"Lefty, we best not tie these horses inside the trailer. We should just let them loose; I think they are too big to turn around in there, so they should be fine."

"It depends on how they haul JR. If they load easy and are quiet, we will let them have their head. If not; we better tie them."

Backing up the pickup truck, JR watched Lefty's hand signals as he guided him under the gooseneck trailer. Lefty lowered the trailer hitch onto the pickup ball; then closed the tail gate.

The horses loaded easily, and once they settled into the trip, were quiet. What JR didn't know, and what Lefty forgot to do, was lock the hitch. Everything went along fine until they got to a steep grade on the freeway, and the horses walked backwards in the trailer. The weight of the unbalanced load made the front of the trailer lift, causing the gooseneck to hitch to pop off the ball, tearing off the tailgate as it rolled backwards down the hill. JR looked in the rearview mirror as the trailer containing the horses rolled backwards to the west, while the pickup was still headed east.

"Dad gummit Lefty, you forgot to lock the hitch onto the ball again!"

Lefty just sat there with a sick look on his face. "I will never understand why I always seem to forget that step."

JR slammed on the brakes and made a U-turn in the middle of the freeway and headed after the wayward trailer with its two one-ton spectators inside.

"That's a well-built trailer JR, notice how it tracks backwards in a straight line?" Lefty said, admiring the craftmanship.

"Who cares Lefty! we have to stop that trailer before it hits a car."

"Speaking of which, you realize you are heading west in the east bound lane, right?"

"How else am I gonna catch that trailer?"

As the pickup truck caught up to the wayward transport, the trailer slowed down on its own, eventually coming to a complete stop; its tires rubbing against a cement curb that functioned as a brake in the nick of time.

Turning the pickup back around, they hastily reconnected the trailer to the tune of semi-trucks honking their horns as they whizzed by.

"You are sooo paying for that tailgate, Lefty."

"Won't be the first time; probably not the last."

Now that the pressure of the crisis was relieved, the boys started laughing about the incident.

"This is gonna make one swell re-ride story, JR."

"Definitely, but we need to embellish it a little. We'll say that the trailer rolled backwards for several miles, dodging cars, and trucks as it went. Let's say that I drove the pickup backwards to chase after it, caught up to it, and you got in the back of the truck and hitched it again while we were still moving."

The two were silent for a few minutes until Lefty spoke up.

"They aren't gonna believe the actual story, JR. For sure, they won't believe the made up one."

"Yeah, you're right. Let's stick to the actual story."

"Except, let's leave out the part about me not locking the hitch."

"Not on your life, pard! I'm telling everyone about that part."

"Fine, and I'll tell everyone the truth about you and Elise Benton."

"You wouldn't dare!"

"You wanna try me? Tell someone about not locking the hitch. See where it gets you."

"Alright, you win ... I'll say that the ball was the wrong size, but we didn't notice."

"Better yet; let's just keep this whole thing to ourselves."

"Done."

"So, if someone asks whether you should tie draft horses inside the trailer or not, JR?"

"Tie them!" the boys shouted in unison.

Continuing their journey, the boys realized they had nowhere to corral the horses.

"There is no way papa Reilly is gonna let us keep these horses at the ranch,"

"I thought about that Lefty, our only other choice is to take them over to Charlie Cooper's place in Deming and see if he will let us board them. Charlie might let us trade shoeing for board."

"Are you kidding JR, that guy is tighter than a Dixie hatband."

"What does that even mean, Lefty?"

"I don't know, I just hear everybody saying it."

"I think it's 'tighter than Dick's hatband', not Dixie."

"That sounds stupid JR, I'm sticking with my version."

Whatever Lefty meant by his Dixie Hatband comment, the truth of the matter was, Cooper was a penny pincher... If it ate, could cost him money in vet bills or maintenance and he didn't own it? He didn't want it. He would never shoe his horses. He trimmed them only when they were almost crippled, and then he would only pay the least he could get away with; but here was the rub. He was a very

Wealthy man. Shelly Travis worked at the bank where Cooper had his accounts. Shelly said that he had almost three million dollars in checking, and ten million in savings.

"Well, let's get this over with Lefty."

JR and Lefty met Charlie at the barn, and after exchanging pleasantries, got down to asking him about boarding the horses.

"Well fellers," Charlie began, "Those horses eat a lot more than a quarter horse. I would have to charge you accordingly."

"That's fair Charlie, care to harden that number a little more?"

"Well JR, I figure they are gonna eat a bale of hay apiece per day. That's three times more than a light horse. So, I guess I would have to charge $30 per day."

"Whew, that is pretty steep, Charlie. That comes out to about $900 per month."

"$900 per month per horse. The $30 is the 'apiece' price."

"I guess we will have to beg off of that deal, Charlie; no way we could pay that."

"I understand, fellers, but if you ever want to sell those horses, you let me know."

JR and Lefty were feeling a little 'hang dog' after hearing what it would cost them to board the horses at Cooper's place. As they were going up the back road to Deming, they went by a house with a sign in front that said, "Horses boarded." Recognizing the owner, the boys went up to talk to Bobby Lara, the owner of the property. After a few minutes of negotiating, Bobby told them he would keep the horses if they would just pay the feed bill. He really wasn't looking to board horses, it's just that his wife had just died, and he was looking for things to keep his mind occupied.

"JR and I will go over to Koenig's and buy a ton of hay and bring it back. That should last a little while."

Jimmy Koenig was married to one of JR's cousins, and so he hoped to get a family discount. Still, hay was selling for $180 per ton at the discount rate, steep if you weren't making any money from the livestock you were feeding. After about an hour, the boys were back with the hay.

"I've never fed this big of a horse JR, any idea how much to feed them?"

"Well Bobby, this hay is pretty well cured, so I guess just feed them free choice. If they are still looking for more after that, I guess give it to them. They might eat a bit more till they fill out but it should level off because they aren't working too hard."

"JR, what do you say we unload them and see if they will work at harness?"

"I thought you would never ask."

Not noticing it before, the team was mismatched. One horse was about 21 hands at the withers, the other about 18 hands. The three-hand difference made the smaller horse a foot shorter than the big one.

"I suspect that these two horses aren't a team."

"My thoughts exactly Lefty. There is no way that these two can pull evenly when they are so different."

"You have any idea which one is on the left and on the right?"

"Trial and error, I guess."

When draft horses are trained, they are trained as a pair. Barring any unforeseen accident or event, the two horses are a team for life; always pulling on the side they were trained to be on. An older draft horse that has lost its mate is one tough animal to retrain.

The obvious difference in the size of the harness made it a simple matter determining what belonged to who.

"I can see the way the reins are crossed that it looks like old Goliath here is on the left, shorty is on the right."

"Looks right JR. What do you say that we get Bobby to saddle a horse just in case we have a runaway?"

"Yeah ... let's not take any chances,"

Bobby had a nice little black and white paint mare that was gentle as the day was long. He saddled the horse with Lefty's gear and tied her to the fence as the boys harnessed the team. Finishing Goliath first, JR took the reins around behind the horse and clucked him into a walk. Suddenly, Goliath got agitated the further away from Shorty they traveled. When he started prancing and bucking, JR knew that shortly there was going to be a rodeo. With a horse weighing between 1,000 and 1,300 pounds, a man could turn the horse's head around and talk him out of running away. A 2,000-pound draft horse barely even notices that anyone is hanging on to them at all ... they sort of just go where they want to go.

"Shut him down JR!"

"I'm trying, but he is gonna run."

Sure enough, no sooner had JR said it, that Goliath took off at a dead run with JR dragging along behind, holding on to the reins as if by some miracle his shouting and swearing was going to make this horse magically stop. Lefty got on the paint mare and ran flat out to catch the horse and the dragging the man.

"Let go of the reins, you idiot! all you are doing is scaring him more."

JR let go of the reins, and Lefty shook out a loop and caught the big horse around the neck, jerked the slack out of the rope, and dallied the rope around the saddle horn. It was when he set the horse up to slow the Belgian down that things didn't go as planned. Instead of stopping, Goliath kept running, pulling the little paint mare off her feet, landing her on her right side while she skidded down the pasture fence line like some sort of equine sled.

Lefty had stayed aboard the horse through the entire episode, and was sitting on the mare's left side, trying to undo the dallied rope that by now was hopelessly half-hitched on the saddle horn. The big horse ran until he came to the corner of the fence and suddenly just stopped and stood there like nothing had happened.

Fearing the worst, Lefty coaxed the little mare onto her feet and looked for damage. Much to his relief, the little mare was unscathed, but Lefty's saddle that he had won at the Las Vegas World Series of Team Roping Championship was chewed up, and the words that he was a Champion Roper embossed on the fender were all but gone. JR came running up to Lefty and the mare to see how bad it was.

"Is she hurt?"

"No, a couple of skinned places. My saddle caught the worst of it."

"Well, that was lucky for sure."

"What the heck do you mean? This is my favorite saddle, all skint up."

"Lefty, between the two of us, we probably have 30 saddles we have won over the years. What's so special about this one?"

"I am shocked to hear you say that Lefty. You really don't remember? Chris Ledoux presented this to me not too long before he died."

Both boys took their hats off and bowed their heads ... Chris Ledoux was their hero.

Sizing up the situation, this Belgian horse deal was turning south in a hurry.

"Lefty, mouth those horses and see how old they are. I have an idea that Goliath is pretty long in the tooth, and Shorty is a lot younger."

Lefty went to the big horse, reached into the corner of his mouth to grab its tongue so he could see his teeth. Experienced horsemen can tell the age of a horse accurately by examining their teeth alone.

"JR, this horse is close to twenty. Galvaynes groove on his upper corner incisor has reached the table margin."

"How about Shorty?"

Lefty went over the Shorty and checked his teeth in the same manner. "He is at least 15, his groove is about halfway."

"You know what JR? somebody saw Mr. Samson coming and stuck him with a mismatched team that won't pull together."

"I got news for you pal, we got stuck the same way, and we are supposed to know what we are doing."

"Let's keep them and try to fix them if we can. Between the two of us, we have had a lot of horse driving experience."

"We will give it a shot, I guess, don't know what else to do."

Time went on, and JR and Lefty got busy doing day work for a rancher West of Deming. Asa Wynn owned a ranch in Texas, and in New Mexico. He had spent the past 30 years raising horses with the color and temperament that suited him. All the horses were a color called Steel Dust; it was a smoky gray color with gold highlights that was very pleasing.

Asa liked a horse who had a little fire but wasn't prone to being crazy. For the past few years, he had relied on the boys to start his newest crop of three-year-old's saddling; JR and Lefty were happy to do it. The first day of work, the boys pulled onto the ranch and proceeded up to the round corral where Asa and his wife Charlotte were waiting.

"Hello Asa, miss Charlotte, glad to see you."

"Good to see you boys, too. How have you been?"

I'm fine sir, but JR here has been sliding downhill. I hope he won't be a burden to you all."

"I see you two are still at it. Better save some of that energy for a project I have for you."

As the four walked to the round pen, the boys could see a black mare with four white stocking feet saddled and Scotch Hobbled, waiting to be ridden.

A Scotch hobble is simply a long soft cotton rope used to tie up a rear leg to immobilize a horse's foot, so it can't kick. Horse trainers use a slight variation of the Scotch Hobble, by tying one end of the rope around the horse's neck in a loose bowline knot, then passing the rope around the pastern of the horse's hind leg, cocking the hind leg off the ground a few inches, and then dallying the free end to the saddle horn. This method keeps a horse from moving and bucking while mounting. When the rider is secure in the saddle, he can loosen the Scotch Hobble from the horn, which usually signals the beginning of the rodeo.

"Wow, she is a beauty. Where did you find her?"

"I had a friend of mine in Texas give her to me JR."

"Must be a good friend Asa, if she rides like she looks, she is worth a ton of money."

"Not to look a gift horse in the mouth, JR, but you kind of hit the nail on the head. Tim Horton, the man who gave her to me, said that he had inherited the mare from one of his cousins who died. Tim is no part of a cowboy, so he called and asked me if I wanted her. I offered to pay, but he wouldn't take any money."

"Curiouser and curiouser JR," Lefty whispered, "something doesn't add up." "What would you like to do with her, Asa?"

"Well, I hoped you would try her out and see where she is at training wise. She wasn't bothered by the saddling or the hobble. By all appearances, she seems pretty broke."

"How was she to load in the trailer?"

"Walked right in Lefty."

"Did you pick up her feet and see if she was ok with that?

"All four, not a problem, JR. She has a suitable set of shoes on her now, so I expect she isn't hard to shoe.

"Lefty, you want to do the honors?"

"With pleasure Asa."

Lefty walked up to the mare and was surprised how tall she was.

"You know, Asa, this mare will fool you. She is so well proportioned that she doesn't look as tall from a distance as she really is."

"I agree, I haven't measured her, but I'm gonna say that she is at least 16 and a half hands."

"Yep, that's about right."

Lefty walked up to the horse and began whispering to her. He rubbed her forehead, and the mare acted like she was happy to be there. Lefty grabbed the reins and pulled the mare's head towards him as he mounted and got set in the saddle. What happened next took everyone by surprise.

The mare was calm right up to where Lefty un-dallied the Scotch hobble and let her hind leg down. As soon as the mare knew she was free, she jumped straight up into the air and the sun fished so quickly that Lefty couldn't keep his seat and went flying, landing on his back.

Instead of stopping like any normal horse would, the mare came after JR and kicked him square in the chest with both hind hooves, and then went hunting for Asa to do the same, but by this time Asa had already climbed the fence and was on the other side.

Lefty was on the ground honking like a goose from having the wind knocked out of him, but he got to safety before the mare came after him as well. Everyone just stood there in dumb silence at the turn of events.

"I guess that answers all the questions we had, doesn't it, boys?"

"Yes sir, I think we understand a lot better why she was free."

"Are you ok JR? Looks like she kicked you into next Tuesday."

"I'm ok … broke a couple ribs. Seems like; long ways from my heart."

"Lefty, you ok son?"

"Embarrassed at honking like a goose in front of miss Charlotte, but otherwise fine."

Instead of calling the game because of injuries, Lefty and JR saddled two of the other colts and took them for a long ride over several miles of southwest New Mexico ranch land.

"You know JR, if we could make a livin' just riding colts, I would sure do it."

"Nobody wants to pay Lefty. We would have to break fifteen heads a month. between us, and you know as well as I do, you can't take on that many horses and do a good job."

" We could go to Texas and get a job starting Colts and make some good money."

"We are New Mexico Cowboys Lefty, bite your tongue."

"You're right. Wishful thinking, I guess."

After a month at the Wynn ranch, the boys went back and checked on their draft horse investment. They were hoping against hope that their feed bill would be manageable, but they knew better than that.

"Hey Bobby, how goes it?"

"I'm good JR, got a bill from Koenig for the hay." JR opened the envelope and his jaw dropped.

"Bobby, this can't be right. Those horses ate $800 of hay in a month?"

"JR, those horses ate four and a half tons of hay. I can account for every bale, and I didn't feed my mare from your stack. I was ordering a ton every week from Jimmy; he couldn't believe it either."

"Dang JR, we can't afford that every month."

"I know Lefty, but we still owe Mr. Samson two shoeing trips. We would have to sell them for $3,200 just to break even."

"Let's go talk to Charlie. Maybe he is still interested in them."

Charlie agreed to buy the horses ... for the feed bill and not a nickel more. Having no other options, they sold the team and all the harness to Charlie for $800. They finished paying Clyde

Samson for the team by trading out shoeing, promising each other never to do that again.

Charlie Cooper fared better than JR and Lefty. He hauled the horses to the Clovis horse sale and swindled someone into buying them for $ 6,000. Small wonder he was rich, and why the boys didn't have two nickels to rub together to make a dime.

CHAPTER 7:
THE BLACK MARE
WITH FOUR WHITE
STOCKING FEET

L efty and JR found work at a dude outfit in Colorado Springs at the Broadmoor Hotel in late winter. For the right price, someone who had never even ridden a horse before could ride the trails on Cheyenne mountain.

The outfit had about sixty head of 'plumb broke' horses that, as long as they were ridden every day, would stay plumb broke and easy to catch. JR and Lefty's job was to haul the horses in from the winter pasture at Castle Rock and get them ready for the coming tourist season. Horses are just like people. When they are working, they slip into a groove and turn into robots. Give a human a vacation for three months and coming back to work is like pulling teeth. The same with horses. Those plumb broke horses I mentioned earlier? They were wilder than the March Hare. Besides the quarter horses, there were four Belgian horses, and a matched pair of black Missouri Fox trotters who were trained to pull a Landau; a sort of Cinderella carriage. The boys caught two of the horses and get them saddled so they could herd the others, except the other horses in the herd wanted nothing to do with being caught. There were no corrals to contain them, just a big 300-acre pasture.

It's times like these where a cowboy has to use brains, instead of brawn, to accomplish the task at hand.

"I have an idea, JR. You notice how this herd has divided itself up into little bands, and each band has a boss horse?"

"Yeah, I see that."

"We don't need to catch all the horses. We only have to catch the lead horse of the band. The others will come running after them."

"Mr. Deutsch said he needed the Draft horses first. Are you saying catch that big blaze faced mare and the others will follow?"

"You know how horses "marry up" and can't stand to be away from each other? I'll bet that if we catch that mare and load her in the trailer, the others will come too."

"Makes sense Lefty, but when you slip a loop over her head, make sure you don't set the horse up like you did at Bobby Lara's place."

"I think I learned my lesson JR, but thanks for the reminder,"

Lefty casually hand signaled JR with a middle finger.

"I'm gonna use that 45-foot Buckaroo rope with the brass honda. I can "long loop" her and then gradually slow her down to a stop."

Roping anything in a pasture differs completely from in a closed arena. In the open, a cowboy has to kind of act like he has no interest in catching what he really wants to catch. When he sees that the animal is relaxed and not looking, he must bust into a lope and throw a quick loop before the animal can react.

Many people think that a big lumbering Draft horse can't run fast. Let me clear that misconception up for you for the last time. A 2,000-pound horse with feet the size of trash- can-lids may be slow at the start, but at full tilt, they are as fast as any horse.

Lefty shook a big loop from the coiled rope and laid both over his saddle horn. The horses were pretty savvy about getting roped. Whenever Lefty had a hand on the lariat, he could see the horses react.

Keeping both hands on the reins, Lefty walked around the herd and pretended to be after another horse just to the right of the big blazed faced mare. When the mare sensed she was not the object of attention, she put her head down and grazed. In one fluid movement, Lefty picked up the rope and let the loop fly, catching the mare before she knew what hit her. As the loop tightened around the horses' neck, she tried to spin and run. Lefty knew better than to stop her with the much smaller horse, so he simply ran along behind her, telling her to "whoa" until she came to a full stop. When the mare started licking her lips, Lefty knew she had quit her nonsense and was ready to be obedient.

"I guess you are expecting a pat on the back, Eh Lefty?"

"Professionals such as I don't accept compliments, JR, neither do Greek gods, or other heroes. You are relieved of that obligation, sir. All you are required to do is feel grateful for the experience, and when you are sitting around the fire with your children and grandchildren, tell them the legend of Lefty Ortiz."

"The only legend I'm gonna tell your kids and grandkids is the story about how you can't remember to lock a gooseneck hitch."

JR knew exactly how to deflate Lefty's oversized ego.

"Alright Lefty let's get a halter on her and tie her up to the front of the trailer.

I'll get out of the way and see if the others will follow her in."

The three horses were pretty cagey. They would walk up to the open gate of the trailer and whinny at the boss mare but wouldn't try to go inside.

"Lefty, this trailer will hold all four Belgian horses, right?"
"Should do... why?"

"I'm gonna tie this gate back with a piggin' string. You get in the truck and start driving off. I'll ride alongside the trailer. and when I say so, you slam on the brakes."

"If this works, JR, I am going to recommend you for a Nobel prize."

Lefty started driving the truck through the pasture with the trailer in tow. As JR suspected, the remaining three Belgian horses started running, trying to keep up with the trailer that was hauling their buddy off. The mare in the trailer was whinnying encouragement to the others.

When JR hollered for Lefty to hit the brakes, the trailer stopped, but all three Belgian horses didn't. They kept running right into the trailer. JR, hand at the ready, pulled the slip knot on the piggin' string, and slammed the gate shut on the wayward horses.

Some people will say that animals don't express emotion because they don't have the facial movement necessary to make faces. But if you had seen the embarrassed look on those Belgian horses' faces when they realized they had been outsmarted; you would change your opinion in a heartbeat.

"That should have never worked," JR said in stunned amazement.

Lefty was whooping and hollering, dancing around the trailer.

"Nobel prize, here we come! It sure shouldn't have worked, but it dang sure did. I call dibs on telling this story first, JR."

"Be my guest Lefty. But how are we gonna get the other horses out of here? No way that will ever work again."

"Deutsch has to have some portable pens. Let's drop these horses off at the Broadmoor and go find some."

Sure enough, Deutsch had more than enough green portable panels to make a catch pen for the rest of the horses. The trailer they were using would accommodate ten heads of light horses, and after six trips; they had completed the first part of the job.

"JR, there is no way that we can ride sixty head of horses enough to get them ready for greenhorns in the time frame Deutsch gave us."

"You know what, Lefty, I agree. There has to be a shortcut we can use to get this done quicker."

"You remember that quarter horse ranch we managed in Gilbert, Arizona, JR? We walked onto a ranch with one hundred head of horses from weanling to two-year-old's who had never even seen a human up close before."

"I remember. That was a job. So, what's your idea?"

"My idea is rather than ride two horses at a time. We do it ten at a time, just like in Arizona. Deutsch has two tons of bagged rock salt for the roads in the winter. I say we load ten heads of horses up with three 50-pound bags and take them on a trail ride."

And so they did.

Tying the string of horses together head to tail like a pack train, the boys could adjust the attitude of the entire herd of horses well within the time allotted to them by Mr. Deutsch.

"I have to say that I am impressed," Mr. Deutsch commented." I know I hired you just for this one job, but I was wondering if you would stay on for the season and manage the whole thing?"

"Well, could you give us a couple of hours to think about it? We have some other commitments that I'm not sure we can move around."

"Sure, take your time, fellers. We are still a couple of weeks away from opening."

JR and Lefty discussed staying on at the dude ranch for the season.

"Pay is not great, but we also have the shoeing work."

"I know JR, but are you sure you want to work with a bunch of dudes? You can't go around punching people out you don't like."

"I have moved past that period in my life, Lefty."

"Really? You just got in a fight a few months back with that cook in T or C., Looks like you forgot to signal before you got past that one."

"What?"

"Nothin', I was just trying to relate what you said to a turn signal. You know when you are gonna pass someone, or get past something, ... you know, pass, past ... kinda the same."

"Lefty, I just lost ten full IQ points listening to that. And I can see smoke coming out of your ears as we speak; your brain is overheated."

"Whatever."

"Well, I vote we stay Lefty."

"I agree, let's do it."

The management job required that both of them not only feed and water the horses twice a day but also oversee four other employees who had very little experience with horses. All of the horses had to be saddled every day and tied in their shaded stalls until they were ready to ride.

The horse barn had 30 stalls on each side with a breezeway down the middle where the horses were fed. The back of the stalls had no gates, and when they needed a horse, they just walked down the breezeway, snapped a lead on the horse and backed him out of the stall. A ski slope was where the horses pastured; yes, I said ski slope. They mostly stayed at the bottom, but a few of the horses would climb the steep hill, so it was harder to catch them.

The solution for this was to only feed them in their stalls, which made sense, but the problem was that there was no perimeter fence around the complex. A horse could take off into the heavily forested side of Cheyenne mountain and be lost.

Now, those afore mentioned Belgian horses were schemers. They didn't work as hard as all the other horses and so they had time to think about ways to escape. Little did those scheming Belgian horses know, but there was absolutely no water in the Cheyenne mountains within several miles of the dude ranch. Horses had escaped into the wilderness more than once in the past and died of thirst after just a few days. If a horse took off, it was the cowboy's responsibility to go after them.

JR and Lefty were born and raised in the flatlands of New Mexico, so the dangers of heavily wooded mountains were something new to them. While they had worked in a few of the National Forest in New Mexico, they never had been in such steep and difficult terrain before. In the mornings, when the gate was opened, and the horses ran to get fed, no one bothered trying to escape for fear of losing a morsel of feed to a rival. In the afternoons and evenings, it was another story. If a horse was called up for duty before it had finished its breakfast, the open stall was fair game for any other horse who was nearby. The Belgian horses, being the cagiest horses in the land, would finish everyone's feed who had been called to work, and by the late afternoon, weren't hungry at all.

One such afternoon, the big Belgian mare with the Blaze's face saw an opportunity as the sun was going down to escape her captors. Lefty, the only one on horseback at the moment, accepted the challenge. Whipping and spurring his mount into action, he ran his horse as fast as he could through the darkening forest. Catching up to the delinquent mare, he spun a loop in his lariat rope and had no sooner thrown it that the lights went out. Lefty came too with a huge knot on his forehead, and no recollection of what had happened.

"Dang Lefty, you ok?" JR asked.

"I'm not sure. Any idea what happened here?"

"You ran full tilt on that little palomino gelding and tried to knock a five-inch tree limb off with your head."

"Did it work?"

"No ... limb is still intact.

"I'll have to try again later. I'm a little woozy at the moment."

"Well, you are the luckiest sucker in the world Lefty, that loop you threw caught the mare, and the slack got caught in a bramble bush and stopped her escape."

"I planned it that way JR, the only part that didn't work was me not being able to knock the limb off."

"Sure pal, whatever you say."

It seemed like every day was full of eager people clamoring to take a ride on a horse. For safety reasons, Deutsch only allowed six riders per trail ride, with one trail guide in the front, and one behind. Because there were only six trail guides, only 18 riders at a time could go on the two-hour ride.

"We have a problem boys, I just booked a major corporation, and we are gonna need at least 50 of the horses to accommodate them."

"I guess I don't see the problem, sir."

"The problem is that all fifty riders have to be finished at the same time. I had to agree to that, or I would have lost the deal."

"Well, how about we put a trail guide every 10 horses, with me in the front and Lefty in the back pushing up stragglers?"

"Do you think you can do that?"

"Yes sir, the horses are all settled in, shouldn't be a problem."

"Good deal then. Oh, I just bought a fresh horse. One of you ought to ride her first before letting anyone else on her. She is in the last stall."

"We'll go look at her directly. We need to get ready for the ride."

JR, Lefty, and the other trail guides made sure each rider's stirrups were adjusted, and that they were clear on how to rein a horse. It really didn't matter, though. These trail horses just followed the horse in front of them and wouldn't respond to the bit, so no actual skill was required. Every now and again, someone who thought he was a horseman would come along; that's when the boys had their fun.

"I'm gonna check out that horse Deutsch bought."

"I'll go with you JR."

As they walked to the last stall of the barn, they saw the haunches of a jet-black horse with two white stocking feet poking out the back of the stall.

"You know what JR, I know it's impossible, but that looks from here like it is that damnable black mare at Wynn's place."

"Son of a buck, Lefty, I think you're right. Please don't tell me Deutsch got bamboozled with that horse."

Against all reason, the boys discovered that sure enuff. It was that same black mare they had encountered at Asa Wynn's ranch just a few months before. To make matters worse, she was the only horse left after the others had been called up for the big ride."

"I'll take her JR. Your ribs are still mending from the last time."

"No, she owes me. I'll take her and make sure she behaves like a lady should."

"JR, do you remember that old broke down cowboy we met up in Carrizozo?"

"Yeah, I'm not sure half of what he told us was true. I think he was full of it."

"Well, that is probably for sure and for certain, but do you remember that piece of 1 x 4 lumber he had between his front and back cinch?"

JR laughed, "oh yeah, he called it a bucking paddle."

"Yep, that's it. Anyway, he claimed that because a horse had to bend in the middle to buck, that stick would keep it from happening. All they could do was crow hop a little. You remember how that mare sun fished and bucked me off? If this thing works, she couldn't do that."

"I'll tell you what, Lefty, anything is worth a try. What did he call it again?"

"A bucking paddle, or bucking stick; somethin' like that."

"Give me a few minutes. I'm going to the shop and make one right now."

Lefty went back to make sure all the horses were ready; JR went to the shop to make the bucking stick.

"Do you remember how this thing ties on Lefty?"

"Drill a couple of holes about five inches from the front, and another two, five inches from the back. Then use a leather string to tie it to the front and back cinch like a cinch hobble. The idea is to fit it, so it hits the horse at the umbilical in the back, and his breastbone in the front. The old cowboy said to be prepared for a weird reaction when she first tries it."

"That's all, no details?"

"No, that's all he said … look out for a weird reaction."

Lefty and JR caught the mare and took her to a small corral where they saddled her and reapplied the Scotch Hobble. They checked the bucking stick to make sure it was secure and in the right place, then JR got on.

Just as she had done with Lefty, she tried to jump straight up in the air. But when she bent her body to sun fish, the piece of lumber poked her in places she had never been poked before. All she could do was stand there straddle legged with her ears back. JR kicked her into a walk, and she started a crow hop that was only a stiff legged bounce. When she realized she couldn't do her usual tricks, the wacky horse started braying like a mule in anger.

Not ready to take anything for granted, JR walked her around to warm her up. In a few minutes, the ornery mare cooperated … JR still didn't let his guard down. Before long, that black and white mare with the four white stocking feet was pretty much acting like she ought to, so JR took the lead and guided the long trail ride up the steep slope of the Cheyenne mountain.

Now, the bucking stick sure prevented a horse from bucking, but the opposite of bucking is rearing, so before they had made it a half a mile up the trail, the mare tried to flip over on JR.

When the mare reared up, JR kicked his foot out of the offside stirrup and as she was going over, he slid off safely to the ground, holding the reins up, preventing her head from banging on the ground. As she gathered her legs to get up, JR was already in the saddle again, securely mounted.

About the third time she reared and flipped over, JR had just about as much as he could stand. On the side of the trail was a length of baling wire that had been doubled and tripled over, making a highly effective quirt. On the fourth attempt to rear, JR over and undered that mare until she stopped.

Now, a horse traveling up an incline has the advantage of gravity when they rear and flip over. But going downhill it was another story. JR wasn't naïve enough to think that the mare was out of tricks. He was, however, a little nervous about what the city slicker trail riders were thinking when he had to "tune-up" the black mare with the baling wire. Every time the mare would blow, the entire trail ride would stop and stare. He could just imagine PETA calling him out for animal abuse.

Well, the mare couldn't do much rearing going downhill. The only thing she could do was curl her nostrils and lay her ears back in anger. JR was grateful that there were no more dustups on the way back to the barn.

"Yee haw cowboy, way to ride," Lefty said as he fanned his hat back and forth like the old bronc riders did. "You sure are the talk of the town, JR."

"Dang Lefty, that mare tried to kill me more times than I care to count. I had to do something."

"Well, Mr. Deutsch wants to see you in the office. Maybe I ought to pack our bags."

JR walked to the office and when he entered the great room of the lodge, all the people on the ride clapped and cheer.

"That was one of the greatest experiences I have ever had," a short, balding man said as he shook JR's hand like he was trying to pump water, "I don't know how you trained that horse to act like that, but it was genius."

"Well ... uh ...er ... thanks, I guess?"

"You made trail ride the best, thank you so much," a blonde-haired lady gushed.

"Thanks folks, glad you liked it. I need to talk with Mr. Deutsch for a minute."

Entering the dude ranch office, Mr. Deutsch was busy pouring over a ledger book.

"JR, I don't know what happened on that trail ride, but I wanted you to come in for your tips."

JR opened the envelope and found 10 crisp 100-dollar bills inside.

"I have to tell you sir, I thought you called me into the office to fire me."

"Fire you?, why would I fire you? I've never seen a happier

bunch of people.

Cowboys like you and Lefty are a dying breed; wish there were more like you."

JR had his fifteen minutes of fame, and Lefty told the re-ride story that got bigger, and bigger, each telling. Not fond of Colorado winters, the boys headed south before the first snow fell, and closed out another chapter of their life.

CHAPTER 8:
THEY STILL HANG RUSTLERS IN NEW MEXICO.

The boys headed to the ranch when they learned that papa Reilly had been shot trying to keep some rustlers from stealing his cattle. They didn't just shoot him, but set his pickup on fire, so he rode horseback the 25 miles to the ranch house with a bullet in his gut. The doctors were amazed that he survived the event; they didn't understand that "True Grit" was not just a John Wayne movie; it actually existed.

The boys were silent on the two-hour trip from Socorro where they had been showing a stable of roping horses. JR's mother was a strong woman, but mama Ortiz had to make the call to let them know about what happened; she was afraid to leave Cillian's side.

Tomas Ortiz, the City Marshall assigned every officer in the department to the investigation. There had been a rash of similar crimes in Luna County; there were still no suspects.

As the pair arrived at the ranch, mama Ortiz was already waiting for them on the front porch.

"How is he, mama Ortiz?"

"He is out of danger mijo, apparently it was a small caliber round shot from a distance so it didn't penetrate too far in. He will have to stay in the hospital for a while because he rode horseback from Los Ojos tank to home; he is suffering from exposure and loss of blood.

"That's twenty-five miles," Lefty blurted out, "I can't believe he rode that far with a bullet in him."

"That area is as remote as it gets. It's a dead zone for cell service, too. Is my mom alright?"

"She is alright, but worried JR. This took all of us by surprise."

"I'll feed the livestock and finish the chores JR, if you want to go to Las Cruces to see papa Reilly it's ok by me."

"Yes, mijo, go see your dad. Lefty can take care of things here."

JR drove the thirty-five miles to Mountain View Hospital in Las Cruces with a lump in his throat. Although he had been the source of concern for his parents over the years because of horse wrecks and such, he had given little thought to the fact that his dad wouldn't be there forever. He and Lefty were both 27 years old now. Neither one of them owned anything except a well-used pickup truck, a bunch of trophy buckles and saddles, and an excellent reputation as horsemen. Most of their friends were married with kids or pursuing some high-powered career somewhere. Both Lefty and JR had not only earned bachelor's degrees, but they also went to Graduate School and had master's degrees in economics; but never used them. JR enjoyed the look on people's faces when they found out about their education; everyone just thought them to be uneducated Red Necks. Lefty was fond of saying that he and JR were the highest educated Red Necks in the world.

Sometimes JR would wake up in the middle of the night and wonder what he was doing with his life. There is something frightening about the early hours of the morning because all the filters are gone from your brain, and you can't lie to yourself about what you have done or what you hadn't done with your life. It's all there right in front of you, and you can't sidestep it or wish it away.

JR parked the pickup in the closest open slot and walked into the hospital. Sitting in the lobby were several of the local ranchers who had been checking on his dad.

"Hello JR, we are sorry for your troubles. I think he will be ok though, at least that's what the doctor says."

"I appreciate that, Mr. Brown. I haven't seen him yet. Lefty and I have been in Socorro working. Just heard about it a few hours ago."

"He is one tough hombre JR," Jim Nance said with admiration. "He will pull out of this and be back in the saddle in no time."

JR excused himself and went to the elevator and pushed the button for the third floor. Stopping at the nurse's station, he identified himself and was directed to the number 2 ICU unit where his dad was. He was not accustomed to seeing his dad in a vulnerable state like he was in now. Tubes and IVs stuck out of his arms and chest, some of them pumping fluid in, some of them pumping fluid out. The scene forced him to accept the fact that his dad was human and not immortal; something that had never crossed his mind before. His mom had been crying, judging from the puffy eyes, and started a fresh round when she saw JR walk into the room.

"Hey dad, what's new?" JR said with a grin.

"Not much son, just enjoying a brief vacation with your mom."

"Pretty fancy Hotel Room. What's it running you?"

"We got the bankruptcy package, a steal at a thousand bucks a day"

"You two stop it! this is not a laughing matter," JR's mom said, stomping her foot.

"Sorry mom, how are you holding up?"

"I'm ok. Did your father tell you he refused to come to the hospital? Did he tell you he was gonna call the Veterinarian and have him take care of it at home?"

"Did you really?" JR said, laughing.

"He rode almost 30 miles with a perforated intestine, and he said it was no big deal!"

"Now honey, it was only 25 miles."

JR's mom glared at Cillian and started to say something but calmed herself, smoothed out the wrinkles in her dress and said," I am going to the cafeteria, I will be back in a few minutes," then strode out of the room in a huff.

"I guess we best stop teasing her dad. I haven't seen her that mad since I wrecked her new car coming home from Lake Valley."

"I have to keep it light, son. If I don't, she gets very depressed when we have troubles."

"I never knew that?"

"She would shoot me if she knew we were talking about it. All those times we got a phone call in the middle of the night telling us you or Lefty got stomped by a bull or slammed into a chute took its toll on her. We were both glad when an entire year went by without you needing a hospital."

"I never knew that it was affecting her that way. I'm sorry dad, I apologize for being such a jerk."

"I was the same way, JR. It just runs in our family. We are all late bloomers, but eventually grow up; that's the good news."

"Can you tell me what happened out there, dad?"

"Well, I was up at Los Ojos tank checking the water when I heard someone driving 4-Wheelers or dirt bikes over the ridge about a half mile away from the tank. I rode up just in time to see five men loading a Semi-truck with our cattle. The cow hauler had a hydraulic system that lowered the entire thing right straight to the ground, so they didn't need a loading chute … amazing invention if you ask me. Well, I came riding up, whipping and spurring that gray colt and took a couple of shots with my.45 Peacemaker. I raised the pistol for another shot and felt something hit me on the right side that knocked me out of the saddle. When I came too, the semi was gone with about twenty cow calf pairs. Here is the weird part; that semi left no tracks, and it looked as though no one had ever been there."

"How did they get those cattle pushed into the catch pen?"

"There was no catch pen. Those cows and calves walked right into that trailer as if they were zombies."

"Seriously, dad?"

"Not a joke son, they loaded like they were machines. How they accomplished it I will never know."

"I think I winged one of them, though; I saw him go down."

JR and his dad visited until his mom returned. He wanted to get back to the ranch and help Lefty. If they had enough daylight, he also wanted to go out to the Los Ojos tank and see if they could find something the others had missed.

Lefty had finished all the chores by the time that JR returned to the ranch, so they loaded a couple horses in the trailer and headed out to Los Ojos to see what they could see.

"Papa, Reilly said that those cattle loaded into some sort of cow hauler trailer that lowered right down to the ground, so they didn't need a loading chute. He also said they loaded like they were pre-programmed to do it."

"That seems impossible to me, JR. That country is so rough, we had to mostly rope and drag them into the trailer whenever we gathered."

"I know, but he was sure of what he saw. Do you know what else? No catch pen."

"Curiouser and curiouser JR."

Arriving at Los Ojos tank, the boys began walking around where his dad said he saw the semi-truck. Starting from about a hundred feet out, they worked their way in an ever-tightening circle towards the middle.

"JR, look at this. I found a tranquilizer dart under this mesquite bush.

"That is weird. If they tranquilized them with Acepromazine or ketamine, they sure wouldn't have acted like zombies. They would have laid down and went to sleep."

"I never heard of a drug that would do what dad described, have you JR?" JR thought for a moment, then a light went on in his head.

"Yes, we have Lefty. Don't you remember what old man Whitaker said about drugs coming out of Mexico?"

"Son of a gun, you're right JR. He said he got those horses to cooperate by using some sort of drug on them."

"We need to tell Papa Ortiz Lefty."

"Yep, my thoughts exactly."

The boys went back to Hatch and walked into the police station where papa Ortiz was busy pouring over mug shots. When the boys walked in, he stood up and hugged both of them tightly.

"You outlaws staying out of trouble?"

"Yes sir papa Ortiz, we have to keep rocks in our pockets just to keep from floating off to heaven."

Ortiz rolled his eyes and laughed. "What can I do for you?"

"We found something out where the cattle were rustled. We didn't touch it and bagged it as evidence."

"Glad to see you remembered something I taught you." Tomas looked at the tranquilizer dart in the bag closely.

"I'll have this dusted for prints; see what we can come up with. Do you have any ideas about what it could mean?"

"Dad, a few months ago, we ran into a man by the name of Whitaker. In talking with him, he told us about a zombie drug that came out of Mexico. He used it on ten head of green horses, and he successfully ponied them for about 10 miles without a dustup. He side stepped the question when I asked him what it was."

"Papa Reilly said that those cows walked into the trailer as if they were zombies. Lefty and I think that this is the drug they were using."

Tomas Ortiz folded his hands and rested his chin on them. This was his thinking pose for serious thought; after a few minutes, he spoke.

"There are a couple of drugs out there that might do what you describe ... one of them is scopolamine."

"What's that, dad?"

"Scopolamine is made from the seeds of a tree called

borrachero. It's mainly produced in Colombia. It's processed into a white powder resembling cocaine. It has a history as a mind control drug, dating clear back to Nazi Germany. Supposedly, the CIA uses it for mind control. I ran across it twice during my career with the DEA."

"So, you think someone is using it to drug cattle, so they just follow each other into the trailer?"

"Either Scopolamine or a variation of it. In a human, 5 to 7 grams will turn them into a zombie, and they will do anything anyone asks. I've heard many stories of people pulling out their life savings and giving it away, then having no recollection of having done it. Ten milligrams cause respiratory failure and death, so it would be quite a trick getting the dosage right."

"Maybe we ought to track down old man Whitaker and ask him some questions."

"I guess you boys haven't heard. They found him last week in a cave somewhere around Trementina. According to the reports I saw, it looked like he OD'd on something. The State Coroner ordered an autopsy; should know something by the end of the week."

Both boys looked at each other in bewilderment.

"Dad, there is no way old man Whitaker took some drug on purpose … the man didn't drink or smoke, much less use drugs"

"How do you know that, may I ask?"

"We have been in the cave. We helped him out with something last year; he was a straight shooter, no way suicidal."

"I'll send this tranquilizer dart to be examined in the FBI laboratory. They can check for a broad spectrum of drugs. It will take a while though … it is the government we are talking about. Meanwhile, I'll let you know about the autopsy of old man

Whitaker. I need to tell you both not to pursue this on your own, but I know I am just wasting my breath. All I ask is that if you run across evidence, that you do what I have taught both of you to do all your lives; maintain chain of custody."

JR and Lefty laughed, then recited from memory the steps to maintain Chain of Custody:

"One ...Limit the number of individuals handling evidence.

Two ... Confirm that all names, identification numbers, and dates are listed on the chain-of-custody documents.

Three ... Ensure that all evidence packaging is properly sealed and marked prior to submission."

"Alright you Smart Aleck's, get out of here. I'm busy."

Tomas Ortiz, and Cillian Reilly had both seen action in the first Gulf War; joining the Marine Corps on the buddy system as soon as they were old enough. They both served three tours in Afghanistan.

Tomas went to work for the DEA after he mustered out of the Marines. Cillian went back home to take over the family ranch. Before Lefty was born, he and Lefty's mother returned home for good. Because of his Law Enforcement experience, Tomas was appointed Town Marshall, and worked directly under the authority of the U.S. Marshall Service.

"Lefty, do you remember those guys over in Deming who were rustling Jimmy Koenig's cattle on the pasture at Copper Kettle?"

"They caught them, didn't they?"

"Caught them but didn't have enough evidence to convict. I think they walked away from the whole deal Scot free. Do you remember their names?"

"They were brothers. Billie Riegert and his brother Fred."

"That's right, I remember now. Couple of scoundrels for sure."

"What are you saying? They are back at it?"

"Just a thought, but it might be a place to start."

"How are they selling those mother cows, JR? The Rockin' R brand we use is pretty hard to alter into something else. That goes for most of the brands in the state."

"I think they are hauling them to Mexico. Someone is building a herd of registered Angus and Hereford cattle by stealing them from American ranchers, I'm sure of it."

Paco Guzman was in a lot of pain. With no access to a qualified surgeon, the .45 caliber bullet in his shoulder was festering and getting infected. He had lost a lot of blood, and a high fever was causing him to hallucinate.

"Can't you shut him up? His screaming and crying are getting on my nerves."

"It's your fault Vato, you told us it was going to be a piece of cake and there would be no shooting."

"How was I to know the rancher would be there? Besides, I killed him for sure."

"You think a little .32 pistol is going to kill something, Henderson? You are freaking delusional."

Henderson was getting angry and had to walk away. He and his crew had stolen over two hundred head of mother cows and calves without incident. It was just his bad luck the rancher was a pretty excellent shot.

He chuckled to himself when he thought of law enforcement scratching their heads in bewilderment, when there were no clues about what had happened. He was meticulous for details;

no one could catch him. But now he had a decision to make. He couldn't let Guzman go to the hospital; they would have to report the gunshot wound to police. He would have to be put down, but he couldn't do it in front of his friends. He would wait until they were all asleep and administer a lethal dose of 230Z.

Eli Henderson had always lived on the edge of the law. He continually looked for an angle in everything he did. Honest folks look at a job or career to help themselves and their employer. He looked at companies and people as his next mark. His entire thought process centered on ways to steal and plunder from others. His selection paradigm for a college major was entirely money motivated. He saw narcotics traffickers making millions of dollars, so he was a chemical engineer. After graduation, he spent years working on designer drugs that would be cheap, easy to produce and highly addictive. One drug he was testing was scopolamine, with a twist. That twist was the synthesized derivative of the Tetrodotoxin producing bacteria found in puffer fish. He had enhanced the mind control properties of the drug he called 230Z this way, making those under its influence completely at his mercy. The downside of the first trials was that those who used the drug ended up brain dead; the price of discovering new drugs, no enormous loss, he thought.

What he needed was a larger test sample that would not raise red flags with law enforcement. The answer to his dilemma came from a great uncle who was looking for a chemical method of gaining control over untrained horses. He felt a little guilty that he had to tie up loose ends.

The first round of testing on horses was amazing. When a

few horses were injected with the drug, they became completely docile. Because horses have a herd mentality, their desire to be close to other horses was enhanced. If you haltered one horse and led him away, the others followed nose to tail like they were … zombies.

A few months ago, Henderson was approached by a wealthy landowner in Mexico about the possibility of crossing registered cattle from the U.S. into the Mexican state of Chihuahua. The Mexican government closed the border to American livestock, so to stock his ranch with the best animals available, he would need an accomplice.

Henderson agreed to cross cattle for $3,000 per cow, and $1,000 per calf, cash on delivery. The ranch owner did not know that he was rustling the cattle he was crossing.

To fool anyone who might recognize the brands of the stolen cattle, Henderson developed a latex patch that disguised the old brand, and another that looked for all the world like a healed over scar of a "made-up" brand.

Using a test herd at the stockyards in Palomas, Mexico, Henderson discovered the exact phenomena he had encountered with the horses. Wild cattle became docile enough to walk up to and put a rope around their neck. They then could be led into a trailer with the others in lockstep; the calves just followed their mommas, making cattle rustling a breeze.

The trailer that they used to haul the stolen livestock had been changed so that through the use of hydraulic pistons, the entire trailer could be lowered onto the ground, eliminating the need for a loading chute. Henderson and his crew would lie in wait early in the mornings at water tanks, then shoot the cows with a 230Z loaded dart from a high-powered tranquilizer gun when they came in for a drink. The drug took full effect in 20 minutes and lasted for three hours. Just the right time to get the herd to their holding pens for last transport.

JR and Lefty traveled to Silver City to talk with the Riegert brothers. There was no reason to believe that there would be trouble, but JR packed his Taurus 9-millimeter with him, just in case. Lefty preferred a Glock 26 for ease of carry. Both boys had concealed carry permits; have to love New Mexico. Driving up to the Riegert's ramshackle mobile home, a huge Pit Bull began barking and snarling at the intruders. The boys learned a long time ago that dogs who barked and snarled were not dangerous. It's those that just stare at you are the ones you better beware of. Walking right past the dog, Lefty knocked on the door of the trailer, and soon a haggard-looking man answered the door.

"Do you remember me, Billie? I'm Lefty Ortiz."

"I remember. What do you want?"

"JR and I had a few questions for you."

"I don't have to talk to you, you aren't the law."

"No, we aren't, but it would be better for you to talk to us, rather than the State Police. There have been more cattle rustling this time at the Reilly ranch. I would like to ask for your help".

"All's I know is it wasn't me or my brother."

"Who was it then?"

"I'm not a snitch ... so even if I knew, I wouldn't say."

JR walked past the guard dog, onto the porch, grabbed the front of Billie Riegert's filthy T-shirt, and picked him up off the ground.

"Someone tried to kill my father. If you know something, and we find out you lied to us about knowing it. I'll come back here and kill you and your brother in your kitchen."

"Look, no need for that. I'm sorry fellers, I'm just scared. Some guy named Henderson is cooking designer drugs in Palomas. Supposedly, he has something that will make cattle walk into a trailer like they were zombies. Hector Perez told us he was looking for some people to help him rustle cattle, but we said we didn't want no part of it."

"Did you hear about a shooting, or anything out of the ordinary?"

"I heard they found Paco Guzman in a ditch between Deming and Columbus. He had a bullet hole in his shoulder, but everyone said it shouldn't have killed him."

"What do they think it was?"

"They said it looked like he OD'd on something, but I knew Paco. He didn't do drugs."

The boys got back in their truck and headed to Deming. JR was still fuming from his encounter with Billie Riegert.

"Kill you in your kitchen, JR? Where the heck did that come from?"

"You remember that Steven Segal movie 'Above the Law?'

"Yeah?"

"I movie quoted Billie Riegert."

"It must have worked. I think he peed his pants."

Lefty dialed his dads' number and soon Tomas Ortiz answered the phone. "Hello mijo, what's new?"

"Dad, we just got through talking to Billie Riegert. He said that someone in Palomas name of Henderson has been cooking designer drugs. One of them is supposed to make cattle act like zombies and load in the trailer by themselves."

"Did he know exactly where he was doing the cooking?"

"He just said in Palomas, I figured there weren't that many places to choose from over there. He also said that they found old Paco Guzman in a ditch south of Deming. He had a bullet wound in his shoulder, but it looked like he OD'd on something."

"Sounds like the same thing that happened to old man Whitaker."

"Our thoughts exactly."

"You boys hold tight until I can get authorization from Immigration and Customs enforcement to take a team into Mexico. You promise you won't try to go there yourself?"

JR looked at Lefty and shook his head yes, "We promise."

"You know what Lefty; I wish we had a supply of that mind control drug for when we come across an ornery animal like that black mare with four white stocking feet."

Lefty was quiet for a minute and responded; "where is the fun in that JR?"

"You're right, my friend, where is the fun in that?"

Later that same night, ICE sent a swat team into Palomas with the sanction of the Mexican government and raided Eli Henderson's laboratory. Henderson had been watching too many movies because when they told him to lay down his weapons, he allegedly cried out, "You'll never take me alive, copper," and so ... they didn't.

Cillian Reilly made a full recovery, and the cattle that Henderson had stolen from him and other ranchers were returned. JR and Lefty hung out at the ranch for a couple more weeks but started getting itchy feet; it was time for a new adventure.

CHAPTER 9: THE LAND DOWN 'UNDA'

Scrolling through an online newspaper one morning, JR ran across a help wanted ad that caused him to perk up.

Wanted: Cowboys to help on an Australian cattle station. Must be able to ride and train rough horses, work long hours, and have weapons experience. We pay top dollar for the right men. Apply online @ www.Aussiestation.org

"Lefty, look at this." "What is it?"

"An ad for ranch help in Australia."

"Dang JR, neither one of us has been further east than Oklahoma City. Why in the heck would we want to go to the other side of the world?"

"Well Lefty, the 'why' starts with an 'A'."

" 'Why' doesn't start with an 'A', JR."

"I know that dimwit just play along. What have we been looking for that starts with an 'A'?"

"Aardvarks?"

"Ok, you are pissing me off!'" "Atlantis?"

"NO!

"Albuquerque?"

"Dad gummit Lefty, you are dumber than a bag of hammers...

the word is ADVENTURE!"

"Why didn't you just say 'adventure' then?"

"Because I didn't know before I started it would be this painful having you guess a word."

"Well … now you know."

"Seriously, let's get online and see what they are offering. We can spend six months down there and see if we like it. If we do, maybe we'll just stay there."

"I don't mind going for six months, but I am a New Mexico kid. Don't want to live anywhere else."

"Fair enough."

When JR went to the link mentioned in the want ads, he discovered that the station would pay for their airfare over, and if they stayed for six months, pay for air fare back.

"Lefty, we are gonna have to jump through a bunch of hoops to get this done. We have to get passports, work permits. Plane tickets."

"JR… you remember old Barney Smythe, that bronc rider from Brisbane?"

"I remember, he was a sure 'enuff cowboy, couldn't understand half of what he was sayin' though"

"Do you think we are gonna have to learn Australian?"

"Lefty, Australian isn't a language. They speak English in Australia."

"Well, how come we couldn't understand Barney then?"

"Ok, I'm done with this conversation. You are giving me a headache."

Lefty enjoyed needling JR. In fact, it was his 'Gomer Pyle' routine that riled JR the most, so Lefty used it every chance he got.

It took the better part of the fall and winter to get everything they needed done. By the middle of December, the boys were boarding a plane at El Paso International Airport for Sydney, Australia, in a blinding snowstorm. Though the flight was mostly uneventful, as usual, JR almost came to blows with a husband whose wife was just a tad too interested in cowboys. Lefty defused the situation by telling the man that JR was a mental patient who had lost his wife in a tragic accident, and he still looked for her everywhere ... it worked.

Almost 24 hours later, JR and Lefty arrived in Sydney, Australia, in the middle of a southern hemisphere heat wave.

"When we left El Paso, it was snowing and 30 degrees outside. We get to Australia and it's 105 degrees in the shade."

"I knew the seasons were different, but this heat and the jet lag have 'put me off my tea', Lefty said, using his best English/ Australian/ New Mexican accent.

"You know Lefty, sometimes it's ok to just shut up, and not say anything."

"Where is the fun in that?"

"Everything doesn't need to be fun. What do you know about fun, anyway? Fun is my department. You know less about fun than you do about anything else."

"It's a fine world, though rich in hardships."

To the amusement of bystanders, both JR and Lefty removed their hats and bowed their heads in reverence, because they both had quoted Captain Augustus McCrae from the movie Lonesome Dove.

Neither of the boys had ever been picky about anything in their lives except three things: their hats, their boots, and their tack. Tack included saddles, headstalls, bits, and spurs. They took a lot of pride in having the best they could afford but couldn't care less about fancy clothes and such.

Now reader, I want you to picture this in your mind. Two American cowboys dressed in boots and hats, waiting at the baggage carousel at the Sydney Kingsford Smith International Airport, as two Wade Roper saddles, two rope bags, two tack bags, and a New Mexico State University backpack come whizzing by. Thinking they had only one shot at retrieving their belongings and fearing that they would lose their gear forever if it went back through the hole, they jumped on the carousel and stayed there until they secured all they had brought with them.

Apparently, Australian Customs officers don't have a sense of humor, so before they knew it, they were both handcuffed and in a holding cell.

"I gotta tell you, mate, I've been in Customs Enforcement for 10 years at this very airport and have seen nothing like what you blokes did."

"We are very sorry, officer. We thought we had only one chance to get our gear before it went back into that hole. This is our first time flying anywhere. That machine that had our stuff on it looked like some sort of shredder or something; didn't mean any harm."

By this time, four burly Australian Customs officers had gathered around the pair of Americans and laughed out loud at JR's explanation of their behavior.

"So according to your work permit here, it says you blokes are headed to the Ranger's Ridge Cattle Station. Is that right?"

"Yes Sir."

"I reckon you still have about 500 kilometers to go before you get where you are goin', so I'm gonna cut you boys some slack and let you go with a warning."

"We appreciate it, sir. Lefty and I have never been in the southern hemisphere before. We would hate to write home and tell our folks we were in prison."

Trying to contain their amusement and not succeeding, the Customs Agents began again to laugh at the strange Americans with the funny accents.

With their troubles solved and gear secured, the boys waited in front of the terminal building for their ride. After almost an hour JR noticed a rundown pickup with the logo for the ranch on the door coming towards them.

"Hop in the Ute fellas. We gotta a long stretch of road and a short time to get there."

"How did you know it was us?" Lefty quizzed.

"You blokes may not know it, but you kinda stick out around here. Billy Allen is the name. Good to meet ya."

"I'm JR Reilly. This sorry lookin' feller is my sidekick Lefty Ortiz."

"Well, you came at just about the hottest time of the year gents, it is hotter than Hades right now. Hope you brought your sunscreen."

"We are from southern New Mexico, so it doesn't seem that bad to us. We are just used to having this in July and not December."

"Never been to the Colonies, so I'll take your word fer it. I thought you came from America? Didn't know you hailed from Mexico."

"New Mexico is a state in the United States, although we live pretty close to the border with old Mexico."

"Well, no matter, I'm the cook on the outfit, I reckon you will answer to one of my mate's name of Barney Smythe. He is the ramrod."

JR and Lefty laughed at the announcement that Barney Smythe was gonna be their boss.

"Me and Lefty rodeoed with Barney a few years ago. We know him well."

"Well, that's good then. I reckon he will be happy to see you blokes. I hear you are gonna be breakin' brumbies?"

"If a brumby is a horse, that's what we signed up for."

"Let me give you a couple of words of wisdom about Australia if you don't mind. Everything here wants to either kill ya or kill ya and eat ya. Ten of the worst snakes in the world are here. Wallabies may look happy to see ya, but they can kick and punch like a mule. You know those cute Koala Bears ya read about? They are a mean lot … best to steer clear of them."

"Well … we appreciate that advice. Even though the weather is the same as home, I have to admit that the trees, bushes, and other greenery are completely different."

"I reckon it's natural to me, never lived anywheres else. You blokes ought a kick back and get a few z's. Work starts bright and early in the morning."

"How long till we get there?"

"We go to bush till we get to that big rock near Urunga. We chuck a leftie, keep goin, and we'll get to Didjabringyabeeralong in the middle of Oonawoopwoop in no time … about five hours.

Kicking back in the Ute for the long ride to the ranch, Lefty laughed to himself about how Australians spoke. 'stick' was 'steek', 'outfit was 'outfeet'.

"JR, you think ole' Barney is gonna make it hard on us because of Tucson?"

"You were the one who teased him the most, Lefty, about that incident. Remember when he went after you in Jackson Hole that time? I think he is probably gonna look for a way to get even."

"Not my fault. He can't fight JR. He started it and I finished it. Besides, he probably has it in for you for sure. Remember when his sister came to visit and rode with us to Albuquerque?"

"Look ... she came on to me. I didn't take advantage of her. She was happy with me when she left to go home."

"Barney wasn't happy JR. One thing you don't do is mess with a man's sister."

"If he was still mad, how come we got the job offer? He being our boss and all. Besides, he owes me from Tucson."

"I think he figures you two are even because of his sister."

"Shut up and get some sleep."

When Barney Smythe first came to the states to ride in the PRCA, JR and Lefty took him under their wing and helped him get settled into American Cowboy life. In the beginning, things were amicable. But as anyone who has ever been around cowboys knows; they are a competitive bunch. Lefty, JR, and Barney all rode saddle bronc, and all three usually figured in the top three or four in every rodeo. It was during the Turquoise Circuit rodeo in Tucson that things came to a head.

Turquoise Circuit rodeo events are those sanctioned by the PRCA in Arizona and New Mexico. Even though there is not a lot of money to be made compared to other professional sports, winning the Turquoise Circuit was a big deal to a cowboy.

At the Tucson Rodeo that year, the boys entered both the team roping and the saddle bronc events. Barney was a pretty fair roper in his own right, even though they don't do a lot of roping in Australia, at least not team roping.

Lefty had asked Barney to warm his rope horse up while he went to pay their entry fees. The Tucson rodeo and the Pima County fair are held at the same time. One attraction at the fair was, of all things ... Ostrich races. As JR and Barney were warming the horses up, the Ostrich race owner came running up to them in a panic. One ostrich had jumped a fence, and the owner was asking Barney and JR to help him. Before JR could answer yay or nay, Barney was off at a full gallop after the errant gigantic bird. JR's idea was to head the bird off and herd it back to the fairgrounds. It was not until Barney started shaking out a loop in his lariat that JR figured out what he was doing.

Now, Lefty's horse was both a team roping, and a calf roping horse. Lefty could use him in both events because he knew what and what not to do when cueing and riding him. A calf horse will slam on the brakes if the rider shifts their weight too far over. This is so that the rider can dismount quickly and tie the calf. A horse trained to team roping will only 'shut down' if you pull on the reins.

JR, riding at full tilt, caught up to Barney and tried to convince him not to rope the Ostrich, but it was too late. Barney threw a long loop that slid neatly over the Ostrich's head, then dallied. In dallying the rope around the horn, Barney made the mistake of shifting his weight too far to the right, and the horse came from a dead run to a screeching halt in an instant, but the Ostrich, and the Ostrich's head ... didn't."

What few people know is that an Ostrich's head is not screwed on as tight as you might think?

As the loop tightened around its neck, and the tension

between the running Ostrich, the stopped horse, and the lariat rope grew to critical mass, the Ostrich's head popped off and shot back over JR and Barney's head like a home run hit by Barry Bonds at Petco Park. The funny thing was that the Ostrich didn't even know its head was gone; It kept running for a quarter of a mile and then finally just fell over.

Barney and JR sat there slack jawed as the impact of what they had done swept over them like a tidal wave. Barney was in the U.S. on what was basically a work permit. One stipulation to keep from getting deported was that they had to strictly obey all laws. JR didn't know what the 'tariff' would be for decapitating an ostrich, but he wasn't willing to take the chance.

"Look Barney, we are far enough from everybody that no one will know who roped the Ostrich. We are gonna say it was me; you get deported and your rodeo days in the U.S. are over."

"It's good on ya, mate, but I own up to what I do. If I'm gonna go for a row, you got Kangaroos in the top paddock if you think I'm gonna wuss out."

"Does that mean no, then?"

"Definitely."

Well, the owner was mad, and just like a cow hit by a car on a back road in New Mexico; it was his prize Ostrich worth thousands of dollars. Before Barney confessed, though, JR piped up and said HE had roped the Ostrich, and that Barney had nothing to do with it.

The Deputy Sheriff told them it was a good thing Barney didn't do it. They had strict orders to deport anybody on a work, or student visa for any infraction, even so much as a speeding ticket. Instead of being grateful though, after the Jackson Hole Rodeo, Barney walked away from the American rodeo forever and went home, messing up his chances for the National Circuit Finals in Kissimmee, Florida that year. Hearing the camp cook tell them who they would work for was the first either JR or Lefty had heard about him for five years.

Arriving late in the night at the ranch, Billy showed them to the bunkhouse, and went to the kitchen to prepare for breakfast just a few short hours away.

Barney Smythe watched from his quarters as the Billy Allen and the Americans drove into camp. He had been prideful about taking the blame for the Ostrich, and it was his pride that caused him to walk away from rodeo in the U.S., but Over the years he softened his stance, and when JR and Lefty's name came up as wanting jobs, he recommended them immediately to the owner. His problem was not with JR anymore. His sister had long since married and packed on more than a few. She was once a pretty girl, but now after three kids and too many snacks; she wouldn't be a distraction to JR anymore.

Barney's problem was with Lefty. Lefty had handed his butt to him in the fight they had; and the memory of it still stung. It was not so much the endless telling of the re-ride story of the Ostrich; it was that Lefty thought he was funny imitating the way he talked. Barney took a lot of pride in being from Australia, and his accent was part of his pride. He had a plan that would teach Lefty a lesson for good; without causing him too much damage.

JR and Lefty had been hired to break and train one hundred head of horses. Barney figured it would take an entire year to get it done properly. JR and Lefty were thinking more of half a year to get the job done. Knowing what the boys were thinking, Barney had rounded up some of the toughest horses in the country. The Ranger's Ridge Ranch started all of their horses when they were four years old and older. While waiting to be trained, they were surviving the harsh Australian terrain and the many dangers it posed. The result was an animal that could not only kick the daylights out of you, but they would bite and strike like a wild BLM horse in the states.

Barney's plan was to make it so they couldn't finish what they started in six months, then they would quit and go home. He could then humiliate them like he was humiliated in Jackson Hole ... at least that was the plan.

"I can't sleep JR; I feel all out of kilter."

"That's because we are 17 hours ahead of New Mexico. We got here a day before we left."

"My noodle is already baked, son; I don't need any more information."

"Papa, Reilly tried to explain jet lag to me; I didn't understand it till now."

"What is it?"

"Jet lag happens when the normal time you sleep and wake up is messed with. You are gonna feel drowsy, tired, irritable, disoriented; but that's pretty normal for you. It's caused by traveling across time zones. The more time zones a person cross in a short period, the more severe the symptoms."

"How many did we cross?" "Probably like 10."

"Not good."

"How was your trip, Billy?"

"Pretty uneventful, boss. Your American friends are gonna feel pretty lousy for a few days. You gonna cut 'em some slack?"

"Nah, I reckon they need to get right to work. I know the times I traveled to the states and back, it was best just to get after it."

"So, is it that Lefty fella that needs a tune up?"

"Ya … he's the one. I reckon I'm gonna enjoy this."

"Did you see those saddles they brought? You reckon Australian horses are gonna tolerate a big western saddle like that?"

"Both these blokes teased me nonstop about my Australian saddle I brought with me. They are gonna find out that they are in for a rodeo strapping that big chunk of leather onto an Australian horse's back."

JR and Lefty heard the triangle ringing that meant that breakfast was ready. Neither one of them could sleep because it was the middle of the day in New Mexico when they arrived at the ranch in the middle of the night.

"I feel like I've been eaten by a coyote and crapped off a cliff."

"Me too, Lefty, but we need to get prepared for what Barney has in store for us."

Walking like drunk men home from the bar, the pair went to the cook shack where the rest of the cowboys were already eating. Barney met them at the door.

"Hello mates, glad to see you both."

"Good to see you too, Barney, although I was a bit surprised when Billy told us you were the rod on this outfit."

"Why is that mate?"

"I figured when you saw us apply for the job that you would reject the offer, glad you didn't."

"That was a long time ago fellas, let's let bygones be bygones, ya?"

"Works for us."

"You boys better get to eatin'. We have a full day ahead.

We are gonna push the horses went want broke to the ranch headquarters, gonna take most of the day.

The boys tried to eat, but they had no appetite. Lefty stuffed some biscuits and bacon in his saddlebag for later. He filled his canteen with water, but it smelled funny.

"This water ok to drink?"

"Why do you ask, mate?

"It smells a little funny to me."

"You'll get used to it. Sulphur is supposed to be good for ya."

Two of the ranch hands led the horses JR and Lefty were going to be using. The boys noticed the cowboys snickering and whispering to each other. Although JR and Lefty had never been on an Aussie horse, they knew their way around horse flesh enough to know what everyone was waiting for.

"They think those horses won't tolerate our roping saddles, JR."

"They are probably right, Lefty. I don't think there will be a problem if we take the back cinch off our saddled. They might object to the feel of it so close to their flanks."

Both boys removed the back cinch, saddled the horses, and rode off without a problem, much to the disappointment of those who bet against JR and Lefty.

"We were hoping for a rodeo JR," Barney laughed.

"I figured you were, hope you didn't lose too much money on that deal."

"Lose? I didn't lose, I won! I bet for you. These boys don't know you like I do. I've never seen any better horsemen, that's why I made sure you got hired."

"We appreciate that Barney. Tell me about these horses we are gonna be workin' Barney?"

"Well, let me give you some background on them. We bring them in, halter break 'em as foals, teach them to stand for trimming, then we turn them back out with the herd until they are three or four years old. But the hundred head you are gonna break are five and six years old. We had a few bad years and they fell through the cracks. These brumbies are stout and won't give up their freedom easily. They are a lot bigger and fully developed than three-and four-year-olds. We have them corralled about a half days ride from here. We will try to herd them back to headquarters so you can use the round pens. I will be honest with you. No one wanted to contract to break these horses. Everyone said they were too old to train."

"You know Barney. Lefty and I have had some challenges with horses. We contracted to break some BLM horses a few years back. I cannot imagine that these horses are any rougher than those."

The boys chatted back and forth with the cowboys, getting to know them better. By the time they reached the place where the horses were corralled, they had become friends.

True to his word, the hundred head they were contracted to break were all sixteen hands and at least 1200 pounds. I have used the term 'break' throughout these pages, but I would like to clarify something. Breaking a horse is actually a misnomer and a carry over from the past. A more accurate term would be to 'gentle' a horse.

Now, a horse is a herd animal. Herd animals exist in a pecking order that begins with the stallion and ends with foals. Every level in a pecking order society has a set of rules that are promptly , and effectively reinforced no matter the situation.

JR and Lefty had the opportunity to work with a Montana

rancher spotting wild horses. The education they came away with was priceless. They learned that you never had to hit or corporally punish a horse. What you did have to do however is make the horse believe that you could pick them up and throw them a few feet if they didn't obey. This establishment of dominance is exactly what is meant by 'pecking order' in a herd. Stallions reinforce their dominance, mares do as well. The most important thing to remember is that it must be consistent. Another valuable insight. When a horse thinks he is hurting itself, they will quit that behavior at once.

For example, JR developed a device called a kicking stick. It was a 2-inch diameter dowl about four feet long wrapped in foam padding.

Race bred colts are hot blooded. In addition to them being hot blooded, they are fed hot feeds. This combination makes for a tough-minded animal. One particular Easy Jet bred filly had a bad kicking habit. She was only six months old, but she could kill a man if she kicked him in the right place.

JR would take the padded dowel and, while holding her by the halter with his left hand, rub it on her hind legs. That , of course made her kick at the 'kicking stick'. They first time she kicked and hit the padded stick with her fetlock, it hurt. After awhile she made the connection that kicking hurt, and she was the cause of the hurt. After reinforcing for a few days, she would not kick to save herself.

JR and Lefty, carrying lariat ropes, went into the big corral to look at all the horses. Both the boys knew that the secret to getting these horses to cooperate was to find the boss stallion and pony him in front of the herd. It did not take long to find out which horse that was.

A solid black stallion that weighed a good 1400 pounds and was almost seventeen hands confronted the boys as they walked through the pen. The aggressive stallion reared and struck out with its front hooves in an effort to intimidate the humans who had dared to enter his realm.

"JR, did you notice that patch on his belly?"

"If you mean that white saddle mark, then the answer is yes."

"You thinking what I'm thinking JR?"

"That horse has enough saddle time on him that he had saddle sores from a girth rubbing him raw Lefty, and it just so happens to be the boss stallion of this herd."

A horse, just like a human, gets a little claustrophobic in certain situations. The boys learned from a famous trainer they met in Oklahoma that if you put a halter on a green horse and try to control him, you are in for a fight. What the boys started doing when starting a colt was to catch a front foot with a lariat, and in no time they could lead that horse around like a lap dog on a leash, and that was exactly what Lefty did. On one of the stallions rearing sessions, Lefty threw a Houlihan loop and caught the big horse on the left front foot. The surprised animal didn't know how to react, so he just stood there, straddle legged sniffing at his hoof with the rope on it.

"Barney, you wouldn't happen to have an extra Australian saddle I could borrow, do you?" Lefty asked.

"Use mine," an overly stimulated Kelly Rigby blurted out.

"Look fellers", Barney spoke up, " I don't think our insurance will cover you riding this stallion. We had intended to leave him here."

" I will bet you our entire wages against you bloke's monthly salary that Lefty can get on that horse and ride him like he was broke." JR hollered.

Barney looked concerned. "Listen mate, this is gettin' out of hand. I don't want anyone getting killed."

"I can do it Barney, piece of cake," Lefty called out.

JR mounted his horse and dallied the lariat attached to the stallions foot around the horn of his saddle and started to walk backwards slowly. As the pressure on the horses front fetlock increased the horse moved forward. JR turned his horse around and started leading the stallion around by his foot with no resistance. After about 30 minutes, Lefty approached the horse with the Aussie saddle, put it on his back, and tightened the girth; the horse still didn't object. Lefty grabbed the pommel of the saddle and jumped aboard the horse... still nothing. When Lefty had a deep seat, JR led the horse around the corral again by his front foot.

"Barney, I need a snaffle bit and headstall." Lefty called out. Barney approached the horse and bitted him, put the headstall over his ears and handed Lefty the reins. JR gave the lariat some slack and Barney took the loop off the stallions front hoof.

Everyone watching that day knew that at any moment this horse was going to break in two and hurt, or maybe kill Lefty, but it didn't. Lefty gave the reins some slack and 'smooched' the horse to move. Without even a bauble, Lefty and the big black stallion trotted around the perimeter of the corral like they had done it their entire lives.

Lefty brought the horse up to where barney and the other cowboys were sitting slack jawed on the fence.

"That is the Dangedest thing I have ever seen in my life Lefty." Barney declared to the other ranch hands. "You boys just witnessed a miracle."

"Ya, a miracle that cost us a month's wages." Rigby moaned.

Lefty looked at JR, and JR looked at Lefty. "We can't take your money fellers. We had secret information that no one else had about that horse." JR explained.

"What do you mean?" Barney quizzed

"Lefty and I saw the Stallion had patches of white hair on his belly that was definitely girth marks from a lot of riding. If we hadn't seen that, there is no way we would have tried to do what we did."

"That is mighty decent of you blokes to say that. You didn't have to you know. Still, a deal is a deal." Barney thrust out his hand to shake Lefty's hand.

Lefty and JR conferred for a moment. "We will let you buy us a steak at an Outback Steak House"

Barney laughed. "Hate to disappoint you boys. Outback is an American restaurant. We don't have them here."

"That being the case then, open the gates Barney, we are gonna have a cross country ride with a hundred head herd of Australian brumbies!"

Lefty took the lead and just as planned, the horses followed the stallion all the way to ranch headquarters. The very next day the boys began starting the horses.

The deal with Barney was that the boys would take the horses from green to rideable. They weren't required to put the finishing touches on their training. The black stallion made it simple to get the cooperation of the other horses. JR would ride the stallion, while Lefty would ride the other horse that was snubbed up to JR's saddle horn.

"JR, we are wearing that black stallion down to the ground."

"I thought so too. How many head do we have left?"

"Just ten head that have not been ridden yet." Lefty announced.

" We are ahead of schedule, anyway, let's give the big horse a rest."

With a few days to spare, the boys finished one hundred head of Australian brumbies in the record time of five months and ten days. As the boys prepared to leave, each of the ranch hands came to shake their hands and express their admiration for an impossible job well done.

JR watched as Lefty quietly when to the Ute that was going to take them to the airport. It was curious that he locked the doors. Lefty was the sentimental sort, so JR figured he did not want anyone to see him all misty eyed.

The Australian cowboys were gathered around Barney watching some sort of video on his smart phone. When they all busted out laughing, pointing fingers at JR, he knew something was up.

Sure enough, Lefty didn't lock himself in the Ute because he was feeling sentimental, he did it because he knew JR was gonna strangle him for showing everyone the YouTube post of him apologizing to Carmen for breaking her heart.

CHAPTER:10 THE COWBOY POETRY OF GARY HULSEY

A good friend of mine has created some great poetry in the cowboy style that I would like to share. He is the kind of man who is true to his word, honest in all his dealings. He will go out of his way to help a friend. He would go the extra mile to save a life.

Gary lives with his wife in Silver City NM. He is one of the last of the old-time cowboys. Reminds me of an old George Jones song, "Who is gonna fill their shoes?"

You can follow Gary Hulsey on his Blog , A View from The Ditch Bank **http://viewfromtheditchbank.blogspot.com**

THE COWBOY AND
THE CATFISH

That a cowboy might stretch the truth a bit

Is a fact we all know well

But when a fisherman tells his story

The facts can really swell

This is about a cowboy named Hank

Who also liked to fish

It seems he wanted to combine the two

He had a secret wish

He wanted to fish from horseback

And he had a lot of hope

He could find a big ol' catfish

And then catch it with a rope

Now ol' Hank he wrangled a few days off

And he headed for the lake

He had a rope made out of Maguey

And it was as limber as a snake

The next day dawned bright and clear

And Hank went riding along the shore

He didn't want just any old fish

It had to be 5 or 6 feet long, Or more

Well, surprisingly he saw several fish

As he rode along that day

But they wasn't what he was looking for

So he let them go on their way

Then a big ol' catfish came lazing along

And it really caught Hank's eye

Occasionally it would make a jump

A trying to catch a fly

Ol' Hank he timed that fishes jumps

He was determined to catch it by heck

Then that fish made just the right jump

And Hank roped it right around the neck

That fish took off like shot from a gun

Headed out into the lake

You'd a thought he was pulling a trio of skier's

From looking at the wake

He was going mighty fast when the rope ran out

And he gave it a good hard yank

Jerked the saddle clear off the horse

And right along with it came Hank

Hank hit the water with his feet stuck out

Using his stirrups like water ski's

It wasn't but just a second or two

He was wet clear past his knees

Then the fish dived for the bottom of the lake

It was pulling ol' Hank right down

Hank knew if he didn't get some air pretty soon

He was sure enough going to drown

So Hank turned loose and headed for shore

As fast as he could paddle

Left that catfish way behind

And it was still dragging his saddle

Hank will tell this story most any time

And he swears it's true and sure

And he don't go fishing anymore

He's got rid of all his lures

But he asks anyone out on the lake

In a motor boat or one with a paddle

If you see that catfish swimming by

Would you try to rescue his saddle.

REVENGE

He loved his cherry chocolates
He bought them by the box
Though they were hidden in his room
He didn't worry about keys and locks
He didn't eat a lot each day
Just one piece, sometimes two
But when he thought the box was half full
He noticed that it was nearly throughHe'd
told the family not to touch
The cherry chocolates belonged to him
But it was obvious someone was pilfering
Some candy on days when he wasn't in
When he confronted his family members
He was met with a strong denial
Since he wouldn't charge them with the theft
And take them to a trial
He wondered just what he could do
As he mulled the problem over for a while
And when he devised himself a plan
His face broke out into a smile
So one day when he was all alone
While tamping down his ire
He took the chocolates and a knife
To the kitchen where there was a fire
With heated knife and a steady hand
He sliced off the bottom of the candy
Then he inserted in an Ex-Lax tab

Then put the bottom back nice and handy
He put the box back in his room
Now all he had to do was wait
For whoever was taking his candy
Knowing how they would meet their fate
He had trouble controlling himself
Wanting to know who was the one
Knowing that when it finally hit
They would head outside on the run
The climax came in a day or two
When his sister made a break
Running often to the outhouse
Cause she had a stomach ache
He told the family there was one more candy
Doctored up in the new box
From that day forward he never worried
About needing to buy any keys or locks.

THE CHASE

It was branding time on the ranch

The corral was full of cattle

While the calves were being branded

Some mother cows wanted to do battle

The corral had been around for a while

The fence was made of pine split rail

It had held cattle for several decades

And it had never been known to fail

The branding continued throughout the day

A couple of young punchers were part of the crew

Helping to rope, flank and brand the calves

They'd been around and knew what to do

The heat was building as the day wore on

The corral was a hot and dusty place

The branding was coming to the end

The crew had dirt and sweat on their face

Some of the cows were getting snorty

And beginning to show their ire

Most of them would follow their calves

As the cowboys roped and drug them to the fire

When the roper caught one of the last calves

It was getting close to the end of the day

As he drug the calf up close to the fire

The mother lowered her head and charged their way

Now those boys knew their life was in peril

As that cow charged for them that day

So they sprinted toward the corral fence

Just hoping to get out of her way

Now that corral was old and the bottom rail

Broke as they hit it in stride

But they were reaching for the second rail

And they did so side by side

That second rail was also weak

And it split, then broke and fell

As they continued their frantic climb

The third rail broke as well

Then the top rail broke and they hit the ground

And they could feel in their mind

The pain that was almost on them

When that cows horns hit them in the behind

They scrambled to their feet and looked around

Trying to find a safe place

Then realized that cow was nowhere near

She had given up the chase

They walked back to help finish up the branding

And tried to put a smile on their face

But they knew that for years to come

Cowboys would tease them about that chase

THE POKER GAME

He'd been a cowboy all his life

Working for thirty a month and found

His pleasures were few and far between

As he worked the years around

He packed a dog-eared card deck in his pocket

Fifty two cards and a joker

He often engaged his saddle pals

In a friendly game of poker

There were some who said he was the best

Some even left the game in a huff

When they found he'd won their hard earned cash

With nothing more than a bluff

A big game was being advertised in town

A tournament of sorts it seems

Open to a total of 25 players

You could get in if you had the means

He made arrangements for some time off

Then he headed into town

To sign his name on the dotted line

And lay his money down

It cost a thousand dollars to buy chips

If you wanted to set in

Play would go until twenty four had lost

As only one could win

The game had been designed

To have a five table set

Five players at each table

And a dealer to track their bets

Lots were drawn, tables assigned

The game had begun

Play would continue until

At each table someone had won

Play seesawed back and forth

Until the coming of the dawn

The cowboys table was the last to finish

And it was the cowboy that had won

The winners stretched cramped muscles

They'd spend the day getting some rest

Then gather again in the evening

And play to see who was the best

When play resumed that evening

A large crowd had gathered round

Side bets were being made

On who would be first to go down

The cards were shuffled, cut, and dealt

The dealer laid down the law

They would play stud, five card or seven

Jacks or better, five card draw

The cowboy started it off quick

He really showed his stuff

By winning the first pot

With a pair of threes and a bluff

The cowboy played very relaxed

The local doctor played the same

The other three players were working hard

Just trying to win the game

There was a lawyer and a merchant

They were playing almost incensed

And a banker from out of town

His demeanor was very tense

Hands were won with houses full

Or with a straight or a flush

With three of a kind or a couple of pair

Or only a queen high and a bluff

The local doctor was the first to lose

The lawyer soon followed him down

That left the cowboy and the merchant

And the banker from out of town

The dance hall girls had since given up

Of getting any one to dance

The men were all gathered round

Watching this game of chance

As play continued through the night

There was a festive air

Among the crown gathered to watch

Who won or lost they seemed not to care

The hour was getting close to dawn

When the merchant finally went broke

The crowd was full of anticipation

The air was thick with smoke

The bankers' chips were getting low

He called for a new deck

"I need to win a hand" he said

"Maybe this will change my luck"

It was the bankers turn to call the game

He said "Maybe I can get even

Let's play a game of stud" he said

"When you deal the cards, deal seven"

The first two cards were dealt face down

And they fell nice and straight

The cowboy drew a ten of spades

The banker drew an eight

Bets were made, the next card dealt

The cowboy drew a spade, a jack

The banker had a pair a showing

He'd drew eights back to back

The banker had the best hand showing

With his eights a pair

His glance at the cowboy told him nothing

He seemed not to have a care

The bankers eyes were turning red

His face was damp with sweat

He ran his fingers through his hair

Then reached up and placed his bet

Though the third card up helped neither one

To win was like a canker

It was starting to affect the actions

Of the put of town banker

The banker liked his fourth card up

It was a third eight

The cowboy got the king of spades

Possible flush or a straight

The last card was dealt face down

The banker knew that it was fate

When he took a peek at his last card

And saw he'd drew the fourth eight

He pushed his chips onto the table

Said, "My eights will bet it all"

The cowboy said "Let's end this game

With all my chips in the pot, I'll call"

There was a ripple through the crowd

And they began to stir

Then they pressed close so they could see

As they sensed the end was near

The banker almost panicked

Then turned over his fourth eight

Said "There's no way you can beat this hand

With just a flush or a straight

The cowboy was a study in nonchalance

Then his smile got very lean

As he turned over his first card

It was a spade, the queen

The realization of what could happen

Turned the bankers expression bleak

Though the cowboys next card was no good

The bankers stomach was feeling weak

As the cowboy turned over his last card

There was shock on the bankers face

"NO" he whispered, "It just can't be"

But it was also a space, the ace

The silence was almost deafening

Then a murmur broke the hush

The cowboy had won the poker game

He's drawn a royal flush

A hand dreamed of by many

But drawn by very few

The banker sat there stricken

He just didn't know what to do

"I couldn't afford to lose this game

I borrowed money to sit in

I've played poker all my life

And I was sure that I would win"

The cowboy looked at him with pity

Said "Some say gambling is a sin

But sin or not there's many who lose

And mighty few that win:

The cowboy said "A rule of gambling

And one that you should choose

Never sit in on a game of chance

If you can't afford to lose."

CROOKED LEG

Crooked leg was a zebra dun

Brought in wild from off the range

He could jump, then spin on a dime

And give you up some change

No one yet had been able to ride him

He gave new meaning to the word rough

Many bronc busters who were good

Ol' crooked leg had shown them not so tough

The kid ask why we called him crooked leg

Because his legs looked nice and straight

We told him it had nothing to do with posture

But more to do with the riders fate

The kid said he thought he could ride him

And he didn't have to beg

We were always willing to give a chance

To whoever wanted to ride Ol' crooked leg

So we told the kid to just climb on

And give Ol' crooked leg a try

When the ride was over we'll explain the name

If he was still wondering why

He put his foot into the stirrup

Then swung gingerly into the kack

Nodded his head that he was ready

Ol' crooked leg humped his back

He left the ground like an explosion

Under his belly you could see the sun

He hit the ground and spun around

The kid was still hanging on

After three more jumps the kid was still there

He was a good rider, there was no doubt

But Ol' crooked leg was just warming up

And the kid was playing out

Still it took two more jumps

And a quick spin around

Before the kid lost his seat

And solidly hit the ground

The kid just lay there for a while

Gulping hard to get some air

Crooked leg looked and him and snorted

Like he was laughing at him lying there

The kid finally caught his breath

But he needed our help to get up

Then needed help to get to the fence

He was walking like a new born pup

We ask the kid if he now understood

Since he was walking so lame

Why all the punchers for miles around

Had given Ol' crooked leg his name.